NIGERIA UNDER SIEGE

FADA

Copyright © 2023 **Fada Publishing**

All rights reserved. No part of this publication may be reproduced, distributed, or transmitted in any form or by any means, including photocopying, recording, or other electronic or mechanical methods, without the prior written permission of the publisher, except in the case of brief quotations embodied in critical reviews and certain other noncommercial uses permitted by copyright law. For permission requests, write to the publisher, addressed "Attention: Book Rights and Permission," at the address below.

Published in the United States of America

ISBN 978-1-961507-99-9 (SC)

Fada Publishing
222 West 6th Street
Suite 400, San Pedro, CA, 90731
www.stellarliterary.com

Order Information and Rights Permission:

Quantity sales. Special discounts might be available on quantity purchases by corporations, associations, and others. For details, contact the publisher at the address above.

For Book Rights Adaptation and other Rights Permission. Call us at toll-free 1-888-945-8513 or send us an email at admin@stellarliterary.com.

Foreword

Nigeria is the most populous black nation on earth with multi-ethnic roots and two major religious beliefs system. Though this multi-ethnic characteristic is similar to some other nations; it is being exploited by Politicians and some of their business cronies for self-gratification purposes. And so Alhaji Abudu, a very wealthy and powerful business man, who made his billions during the Nigerian Civil war, hatches a plot to return the country back to a civil crisis to sell arms and recoup the money he lost in a bad investment. Alhaji teams up with his old friend Lawani, an ex-military general and together they're set to plunge the most populous black nation into an unprecedented refugee crisis in the history of Africa. But his plans are about to go South with the kidnapping of Bisi's fiancée- Ayo. As the suspicions and intrigues unfold, Alhaji Abudu discovered that he would need more than the secret organizations he initially relied on to create havoc in Nigeria and its people.

Acknowledgement

To the best dad ever, David .I.P Obode (an author) and my lecturer, Dr. Godfrey Obetoh who helped me develop my Sociological imagination.

Dedication

This book is dedicated to my wife and sisters.

Contents

Foreword iii
Acknowledgement iv
Dedication v
Chapter One 1
Chapter Two 9
Chapter Three 21
Chapter Four 29
Chapter Five 38
Chapter Six 48
Chapter Seven 57
Chapter Eight 65
Chapter Nine 76
Chapter Ten 88
Chapter Eleven 95
Chapter Twelve 104
Chapter Thirteen 120
Chapter Fourteen 130
Chapter Fifteen 137

CHAPTER ONE

Jegbefo Osemudiamen woke up with a start thinking he heard a noise, slowly he rolled over and peeped at the clock on his bed; it was 2.25am in the morning. He muttered something under his breath and sat up. The noise came again, this time a bit louder.

For the past eight years, he had been a good cop that was respected by colleagues and those in authority. He is the one that gets the job done when others failed; he was different from the lot. He has been so trained that he can even hear the minutest suppressed sound; Jeg, as his friends would call him, was the best officer the Edo state police has ever had.

Jegbefo was in his early 30s, a 6.1" feet tall with broad shoulders and a face that always smiles hence his friends called him 'Jeg the smiles'. Hearing the sound again, he slipped out of his bed pulling his .45 colt automatic from under the pillow. This time he was sure the noise was that of a car.

'damitt' he murmured. 'What will a car be doing here by this time in the morning'.

Moving fast but silently, he tip toed to the window; raised the .45 automatic above his shoulders and slightly pulled the blinds down with his other free hand, the powerful security lights outside gave him the picture of a parked BMW 5 series car outside the gates, with the parking lights on. He moved to the next window to get a better view and from there he saw three men standing by the car. He could see one was huge and thick, the second was lanky while the third one was short and stout. But Jegbefo had seen the huge guy somewhere before. He searched his brain to remember but could not.

The men were now heading for the flat next to him; the two men were behind while Mr. huge led the way. Jeg now remembered him; he had run into Mr. Huge when he was caught with his girlfriend some months ago. Jegbefo who could not fight back because he was not supposed to be in that place was beaten up and thrown out. He had wanted some information from the girl concerning a murder case. He shoved the thought off and brought his mind back to the car which he identified as a BMW with registration Dk 9804 FAK.

Suddenly, his mind flashed to is neighbour Bisi! The three men were already inside her apartment which was about 50 feet away from his flat. Smiling cheerfully as if he just got a promotion, he went back to his bed, took out his silencer from the drawer by the bed and screwed it to the .45 automatic. By this time, he was chuckling. He always enjoyed things like this. He went back to the window but the men had not appeared. He rushed to the back door, opened it, quietly got out and closed it behind him. As he raced towards the other flat, he stopped dead when he saw them coming out of the apartment. Bisi was being dragged by the two men who gagged her, her hands tied to her back. Mr. Huge was behind them now with his hands tucked deep into his pockets.

Jegbefo quickly lurked behind a flower and studied the situation. As they approached the gates, Bisi began struggling with them. Jeg moved forward lurking in the shadows. These men were sure kidnappers he thought. He either stops them or they make away with the girl.

From his hideout, he raised the .45 and aimed knowing he never miss his target; the gun hissed twice and Mr. huge gave a muzzled groan and jerked backward immediately. He quickly aimed again and squeezed the trigger before Mr. Huge hit the ground. The bullet tore through the lanky man's throat releasing streams of blood everywhere. He let go of Bisi and held on to his throat, struggling for air while applying pressure on it but there was nothing he could do about it; the slug had passed through the spinal cord, he fell forward and spread out on the grass. The stout man came to an abrupt halt and looked back, apart from the girl, the songs of the insects and the powerful street lights, he was alone. Bisi began to struggle fiercely from his vice grip; confused and bewildered, the stout man hit her on her face and drew out his

.45 colt automatic with a cone shaped silencer. He began to fire the gun sporadically and with his left hand, drag her on the ground; then he hurriedly made for the car that was about 30 feet away but he never made it. Jegbefo shot him on his head; he let go of Bisi as he jumped, bawled and danced in the air before hitting the ground.

Hearing the shout, the driver inside the BMW quickly turned his head towards were the shout came from just in time to see the stout man falling. He looked round but saw nobody; he quickly engaged the gear, swung the car round and headed east cursing as he fired the car through the deserted upper mission road. Jegbefo ran after the car and fired shots at it but that didn't stop the driver. He stood as he watched the car fade away into the night. He cursed himself for not thinking about the driver. He would have first taken care of the driver he thought; he looked round but couldn't see Bisi, she must have run back to her apartment, he quickly crossed the gates and went to meet her. The front door was open, so he entered the balcony, crossed the living room and searched the rooms but she wasn't there. He then went to the kitchen and met her struggling with a knife to cut herself loose. Her pale face with a patch where the stout man had hit her lighted up when she saw Jegbefo. He came close to her, cut her loose and removed the gag from her mouth. Both of them stood for some moments looking at each other.

'May I use your phone'? He finally said breaking the silence.

'Of……of course' she stammered

Jegbefo went back to the living room raised the receiver and dialed headquarters. Sergeant Osaro responded almost immediately the phone rang.

'This is Edo State police headquarters'.

'Hello Osaro, it's me Jegbefo, put me through to the chief'. After a long delay that seems like an eternity, a deep rich voice called out.

'Yes'?

'Three fat eggs have just been laid outside my apartment'. There was a brief pause, then;

'We'll be there in 7 mins'. And the line went dead. Jeg dropped the receiver and wondered why one would have to call headquarters before speaking to the chief that was at home. He shrugged the thought of him and returned to the kitchen. Bisi was still standing where he had left her; her face white with fear. He grinned, went to the bar in the living room and came back with a bottle of whisky and a glass. He poured some into the glass and gave her. She grabbed it with her two hands and took it in a gulp. Jeg poured her another and led her to the living room.

'Sit down' he said. She obeyed, he went to the front door which was still opened, closed it and came to sit opposite her.

'I will want you to put yourself together and calm down okay?' Bisi just nodded her head, gulped the remaining whisky in the glass and set it down carefully on the stool beside the sofa.

'Am going out there to look the corpse over….'

'Please don't leave me here' Bisi protested getting up.

'No! You just sit down here and relax' and before she could say another word, Jegbefo was already outside. He took quick steps towards the corpse but the chief and his escort were already driving into the compound. Jegbefo hurried and open the door for the chief.

'Ok Jeg,' the chief started, climbing out of the car, 'what happened here?'

Quickly Jegbefo narrated all that happened. When he was through, the chief turned to the officer, standing beside him;

'Get an ambulance'. And turning back to Jegbefo,

'Where is she now'?

'In her apartment'.

Jegbefo replied leading the chief to the flat. He ushered the chief inside the living room. Bisi was in control of herself now.

'Bisi, meet Mr. Latif, the Commissioner of police in Edo state'. Nodding the chief selected a chair and carefully sat down on one that creaked under his weight. Mr. Latif is a fat and tall hairy man. Despite his weight, he was always alert when it comes to performing his duties.

'We are very sorry about what just happened but if you don't mind, I will like to ask you one or two questions. Jegbefo glanced at her but she was silent. He turned to the door open it and went out to meet the ambulance that had just come in.

The chief looked at Bisi firmly and asked, 'Do you have an idea of what just happened'?

'No' she said abruptly

'How did they get into your apartment'?

'I think through the back door, the kitchen or something. Really don't know now '

'do you have any idea why they came for you'?

'Sir I appreciate you and Jegbefo for the assistance given me but outside that I can't help you, please'.

'Take it easy'

the chief said surprised his voice was still calm. This discussion was not leading anywhere and he could sense Bisi was not willing to co-operate.

'we need to ask you some questions to enable us track down these people; if you are not giving us anything, then it would be difficult to track the people after you'.

'Am terribly sorry sir but I don't have the information you need'.

Bisi got up, walked to the front door and held it wide open.

'All you can do for me is to get rid of the corpses outside'

The chief causally glanced at his gold wrist watch that read 2.58am. He got up slowly, shrugged his shoulders and stepped outside. The ambulance was just driving out and Jegbefo was rushing back when he saw the chief descending the short staircase.

'Come with me to the office' the chief said quietly. The four minutes' drive to the office was silent. They got to headquarters and went upstairs straight to the chief office. Inside the chief office, he told Jegbefo how his discussion with Bisi had gone.

'So what do you think'? The chief asked

Jegbefo relaxed in his seat and yawn. 'I have seen the huge guy before; you remember that murder case where a whole family was wiped out last year'? The chief nodded.

'Somehow' Jegbefo went on, 'this huge guy was involved but I just couldn't connect him with the case; so he slipped away just like that'.

The chief stared at Jegbefo for some time and then lifted the receiver.

'I want detective Ubani and Akpan here now and I mean now'. He dropped the receiver and turned to Jegbefo.

'I want you to dig into this huge guy or whatever his fucking name is. I want to know everything about him, his family where he has lived for the past 12 years and you have seven hours'

Jegbefo got up and went out, he nodded to detective Ubani and Akpan as he passed them on the stairs case.

As Mohammed heard the stout man shout and saw him falling down, he quickly swung the car round and headed for the Kings square. The shots that were fired towards him shattered the back glass and one of the shots narrowly missed his head as it tore part of the head rest. He raced the BMW down the quite upper mission road without the headlights using his parking lights and the streets light while looking back frequently to see if he was been chased or followed. The whole operation has failed he thought, that gun man was sure a hell of a shooter. Even Owa who Lawani trusted so much must have been killed. He wondered how he would relate the message to Lawani , this was the first time an operation carried out by their team failed. He cursed himself for being pre-occupied with the movie he was watching inside the car. He would have to dump the car and go back to Kaduna with the helicopter that was waiting for them. He was now doing 160km/hr. as he crossed the New Benin market traffic light without stopping after all, the road was completely deserted.

'Mr. Lawani would give……' he let the word go. He wasn't going to think about that. As he passed Emokpe primary school, he called the pilot. Mohammed began to slow the car down as he approached the king's square, he sighted the chopper waiting with the engine running; he looked back again and became a bit relaxed. They had come all the way from Kaduna with the car but they had planned for the chopper in case of emergencies such as this.

He stopped the car about 5 feet away from the chopper, got out and climbed into the chopper as it took off immediately.

'What happened'? the pilot asked

'They didn't make it'

'You mean Owa, Meenne and Diunu are dead'?

'You heard me, didn't you, or is something in your ears'?

The pilot turned to look at Mohammed but the look in his eyes sent a cold chill into him, he quickly turned his attention to the controls and increased the chopper's speed. Sixty-five minutes later, they were in Kaduna. A black land rover was already waiting; Mohammed got off the chopper and entered the SUV. They drove in silence and when it pulled up in the Hotel de' Plazaen, Mohammed got out and took the lift to the seventh floor.

'Where is your team'? Lawani asked

'They didn't make it' Mohammed said shutting the door of Lawani's office.

'What do you mean they did not make it'?

Mohammed walked gently into the office, pulled up a chair and sat down. He then told Lawani what he saw and how he had to run away. Lawani was bewildered. What and how in hell did this happen to one of his best team; he wondered how he would relate the sad news to Alhaji. He thought for some time and then asked.

'What happened to the girl'?

Sir, I don't know, when I saw Diunu shot and the others were no were to be found, I scrammed '.

'Okay' Lawani said, weaving him away with his hand. Immediately Mohammed stepped out, he started thinking; from dusk to dawn they had looked for Bisi but now that they had found her, she just slipped away from their hands at the expense of some of his best men; Lawani wondered if his men had walked into a trap. Bisi now knows that she is a wanted person, this will make her more cautious but what if she goes straight to the police? He thought, what if she tells them what was cooking? Well that would be it. But what if she doesn't know about what is going on, of course that will give them plenty of time. Lawani stretched out his legs and stared into an empty space. What if Bisi had already gotten wind of the disappearance of her finance? She could go straight to the Federal Government with her connections and tell them that a coup is on its way. He got up and moved to the door marked 'PRIVATE'.

'Alhaji would have to hear this'. He said to himself.

CHAPTER TWO

Mr. Latif's office is not too big. He was that type that didn't care much about luxury in the office apartment. His large desk was between the window and the door. There are four other chairs reserved for visitors facing the desk. The wall clock stood at 12.05pm. Jeg was sitting down to the chief's left while detective Ubani and Akpan where to his right waiting for the chief who was on the line. He was looking troubled as his dream has always been to keep a record of a very low crime rate in whatever state he is posted to.

'Yes gentlemen', he said dropping the receiver. 'fill me up'.

Jegbefo sat up, put his file on the desk and told him how far he had gone.

'Mr. huge' he started, 'has neither friends nor relations. His name is Owa Omoruyi. He is a dedicated killer and his last official job was the assassination of the Kogi state Commissioner of police and his deputy last year.' Jeg paused as the chief opened the file and continued;

'Owa has a criminal record with Abuja, Lagos, Kano, Kogi and Rivers states police command but none of them has been able to lay their hands on him as he has not been seen for over 10 months until yesterday'.

Mr. Latif nodded and asked,

'when did you say you first saw him'?

'Eleven months ago sir'. The Chief relaxed, he lit a cigar, inhaled deeply and puffed the smoke into the air, Jeg looked away. He had always told the chief that cigar is harmful to his health and the chief had always promised to quit; it was more of a chronic habit for Chief Latif.

'What have you got Akpan'?

The chief asked without looking at him. Like Jeg, Akpan dropped his report on the desk and narrated his.

'The car that was used is a BMW 5 series car with registration number DK 9804FA……..'

'That's what I told the chief' Jeg said cutting him short.

'Keep talking Akpan', the chief said puffing out smoke from his nostrils, 'am listening'

'The car was dumped at the kings square and the lab boys have worked on it but there are no prints. The interesting thing is that the car was initially stolen from one Mallam Dawodu in Yobe state who had declared the car missing over three months ago now'.

Akpan paused and looked at Jeg with a grin and continued.

'I quizzed all the banks security men around the King's square on duty last night and seven of them swore they saw a chopper parked at the entrance to the museum for more than 30 minutes before the BMW came and the pilot took off in so much haste'. I think the chopper was getaway mobility for them. I have also tried to check the airport but there is no record of the chopper ever entering the Benin air space.'

The chief puff some more carbon into the air and asked;

'Where is the car now'?

'Down stairs sir'

Mr. Latif picked up Akpan's report and flip through.

'what about you Ubani' he asked looking at him directly.

'the other two men Meenne and Diunu are foreigners' Ubani said happy with himself

'although they were carrying the National ID and the Nigerian taxpayer identification card, investigation has shown that they are not Nigerians'.

'were did they come from'? Jeg asked causally.

'that's the question I have been trying to answer. But from their facial appearance, they look like Malians to me. I strongly believe that they came in through the land border as there are no records of them entering through the airports'.

'well gentlemen' the chief said crushing his cigar in the ash tray, 'the divisional police officer in charge of New Benin police station covering the area where the crime scene occurred was in my office this morning and we have discussed. I told him we'll handle the case from here but Akpan will have to fill him in'.

Akpan nodded his head and asked

'what next chief'?

Chief Latif relaxed back his chair and said;

'whoever we are dealing with is sure desperate to get a hold on Bisi at all cost. In the meantime, we need to go low on this one. But I want you Ubani to check with the immigrations if they have any records of these two'.

'yes sir' Ubani said standing up.

'Jeg, I need you to put a guard in Bisi's place to watch her. And as for you Akpan, liaise with the Yobe Police command and see if you can have a lead on that'.

'Excuse me chief', Jeg started; 'Bisi would not have someone guarding her. I discussed with her and she was very straight on it'.

The room was silent and after some minutes, Ubani broke the silence.

'I think this girl is crazy; first she snub's the chief and now she doesn't want protection? Who the hell is she anyway?'

The chief got up, walked towards the window and took a deep breath then turned to face them.

'Bisi is well connected. She goes way up to the Presidency so care must be taken in handling her. So, Jeg, just put a man in the shadows to watch her while Akpan walks with the New Benin police division and Yobe to get a lead. As for you Jeg, maintain your normal friendship with her, until we see where this thing leads. I don't want anybody spoiling my state'.

Lawani tapped on the automatic door marked 'PRIVATE'. The doors immediately open and closed again as he stepped into his boss office. The office was large and well furnished with paintings, portrait pictures and quality leather chairs. The P.O.P ceilings had elaborately decorated designs covered with orange paintings; and the deluxe room contained two big chairs facing the desk that was big enough to play snookers on.

Alhaji Abudu was standing by the window, staring at empty space. He didn't look back when Lawani entered. No one could enter like that apart from him. Lawani crossed the big room and came to seat in one of the chairs.

'did you get the girl'?

'am afraid not Alhaji'

'what do you mean'? Alhaji snarled bringing his face to look at Lawani.

'where are the boys now'?

'Dead, except the driver'.

'How did it happen'?

Alhaji asked coming to seat behind his desk. Lawani told him what Mohammed had told him. When he finished Alhaji opened one of the gold boxes on the desk and brought out two of his home made cigars, he offered one to Lawani who gladly accepted. They both lit up and smoked in silence. Alhaji was awakened by the news. This team was his hit squad and he wondered how they lost them just like that. Alhaji knows they can't start losing men so early; he began to think of the next move.

'Okay' he finally said. 'Let's leave the girl alone for now and face other important matters. I will be leaving for Senegal tomorrow morning to see an organization about some pressing issues. Meanwhile, I have arranged that Bamidele leave for Togo this evening. An organization with links to the government is giving us seven modern tanks worth over 20 million dollars in exchange for oil'.

'who's making the first delivery'?

'they of course' Alhaji said getting up. He crossed the room to the wall painting by the window and removed the picture covering the safe buried inside the wall. He opened it, brought out some papers and returned to his chair.

'go through this' he said pushing the papers to Lawani.

He went through it, raised his head and grinned. The papers contained the agreement between Alhaji and the organization named Kawasaki.

'the funny thing there' Alhaji went on 'is that we do not have oil to give. So immediately the tanks are delivered, we go underground'.

Lawani's teeth were all white. He has known his boss for a very long time now. He was the type of person that was quick tempered, dubious, cruel and never kept his word. But the world has only known a good and successful business man. As soon as they get the tanks, they will say goodbye to Kawasaki and the Togolese government and that will be it.

'all I need you to do now' Alhaji continued collecting the papers, 'is to smuggle the tanks into the country and wipe out any trace that could lead them to us'.

'that will be like serving tea Alhaji, leave me to that'.

Alhaji nodded his approval.

'there will be no need for us to use this office anymore because they already know here so start parking'.

'to where'?

'To the **plaza de Richie in Yola**'. All the necessary arrangements have been made just liaise with the manager'. He got up and returned the papers back to the safe.

'How long will you be staying in Senegal'?

'Four days, maybe less depending on the arrangements there'. Alhaji walked towards the window, and Lawani stood up knowing that the discussion was over. He came back to his office, walked to his desk and lifted the red telephone receiver.

'Call me the Cleaners' he said and replaced the receiver. He sat down and raised the black telephone receiver. He dialed six digits and said;

'Send Obakpolor to Benin to watch Bisi. He should not have anything to do with her just to monitor her movement and give his daily report'.

'Yes sir', the voice at the other end said. 'Is there anything more'?

'No' Lawani said and hang up. He was going to wait for the Cleaners before he broke the news that they were packing. He raised the black receiver again and dialed three digits.

'Put me through to Chief Adeyemi'

'Wait a moment' the operator said and after a brief delay, the chief voice came alive on the line.

'Yes Lawani, is this line clean'?

'Yes, it's clean. I have an important job for you, can we meet'?

'Ahhh.... Let's see, I think I will be available in two days' time'

'That's fine I will be in your house by 9pm two days from now, is that ok'?

'Sure, I will be home'. Lawani hang up and relaxed. The Chief of customs in the country has always co-operated with them after all, what was he being paid for? Alhaji had made sure that some top officials were under his pay roll to facilitate their plans. The intercom buzz and he leaned forward to answer it.

'Yes!'

'Mr. Bamidele is here sir' the secretary said

'Send him in'.

Some few minutes later, a tap came on his door.

'Come in' he said. The door swung open and Bamidele stepped in.

Bamidele is about 6.3" feet tall, with an athletic appearance. His smooth light completion skin is what the ladies find difficult to overlook and that was one of the problems that he finds himself always dealing with. Dele as he is popularly called, believes one cannot survive without money. He was in his early thirties and lives a life style that usually attracted girls.

'Sit down' Lawani said. Dele went to his favorite chair and sat on it. Lawani pushed a case of cigar towards him.

'Help yourself' he said. Dele leaned forward, selected a cigar and lit it; he dragged nicotine into his lungs and released the smoke almost immediately.

'Alhaji said you want to see me'. He said as he used his hand to blow away the clouds of smoke that made him not to see Lawani clearly. Lawani sat up and remove the case of cigar before Dele could reach for another one.

'you have been informed of your trip to Togo'?

'yes. Its two hours from now'.

'I trust you've packed and been told what to do'?

'yes! but there is one thing. Alhaji said I should represent him there. All I have to do is make the negotiations and the tanks will be released. How do I get them into the country'?

Leave that to me'. Lawani said feeling superior. 'I have already arranged that.' The intercom buzz and he leaned forward to answer it.

'yes'?

'the cleaners are here sir'

'Send them in'.

'they are already on their way up'.

'ok' Lawani said and almost immediately, the door opened. Two fat men entered and sat down nodding to Bamidele.

'Sorry I had to call you off' Lawani said

'no problem boss'. One of them said. Lawani turned back to Bamidele;

'I want you to make sure that no body follows you back cos' we aren't keeping our side of the bargain; and besides we are moving from here to Yola.'

'that might be a bit of a problem you know that.'

'just make sure you come back alone and clean too. Is that much of a problem for you to handle'? Lawani was now raising his voice feeling irritated by Dele's comment.

'And don't try anything funny while there. Remember we still have a chip inside you. If anything goes wrong, your sister would pay the price'

Bamidele clenched his fist where he sat, his face very straight but expressionless.

'well', he started, fighting to keep his voice calm. 'I don't think it has gotten to that, I was just trying to raise.......' Lawani raised his hand to cut him off. He turned to the cleaners;

'we are moving out of here to plaza de Richie in Yola. So I want you two to clear and clean all traces that we ever stayed here understood.'

He paused to bring out a homemade wine from his drawer, poured himself a drink and emptied the spirit in a gulp. He swallowed hard with a twisted face and set the glass carefully on the desk.

'we'll be leaving with the two helicopters at 2300 hours tomorrow, so start packing.' The cleaners stood up and hurried out of the office. Lawani beckoned to Dele who followed him into Alhaji's office.

Bisi Adebayo came out of the Oba market. She looked round the crowded area trying to place where she parked her car. She smiled and headed towards it when she sported the Rav 4 SUV. Bisi just twenty-nine is slim, light completion and tall with natural blonde hair, a mild large but firm breast and a narrow waist fitted into an intimidating solid and protruding hips. Her long lovely legs and her brown sexy eyes with light eyelashes made it impossible for her to go unnoticed. Even her constant smiling posture sometimes gave guys the wrong impression.

She dropped her shopping bags in the back seat, got behind the wheels and started the car. As she drove out of the parking lot, she turned right heading for Obakhavbaye road so as to connect the Ugbowo Lagos road; unknown to her that she was been followed by a Honda CRV. Bisi had parked out of her former apartment when Jegbefo her former neighbour went on leave. As she approached the Oroghene junction, she saw her friend Ufan waving her from the side walk and Bisi squeezed the Rav 4 in between a Honda pilot and a Volvo car, pulled up near the side drain and Ufan jumped in as the Rav 4 speed off.

'whaaaoooooo, that was some driving girl'.

'where have you been' Bisi asked 'I tried calling you before I went shopping'.

'I dropped my car with the mechanic then came to the bank to pay some bills'.

Ufan was now looking into the shopping back in the back seat.

'I will be free tomorrow, we need to talk'

'what's up girl'?

'plenty dear, when you come around tomorrow, we'll talk'.

Bisi slowed the car down as she approached 13th street in the BDPA estate. She cleared off the road and Ufan got out.

'see you tomorrow evening' Ufan said and closed the door.

Bisi engaged gear and drove home. On getting home, she carried the shopping bag inside the kitchen and arranged them inside the fridge. She took her bath, ate and went round the rooms in her naked figure.

'damit' she muttered under her breath, 'I forgot to attend the dinner invitation of the Iyohas'.

She walked briskly into her room and went straight to the widow; she looked outside, leaned forward to pull the glass in and locked it. It was getting dark now and the wall clock told her it was past 7pm. She switched on the air conditioner with the remote, picked up her cell phone and collapse on the bed. Reluctantly, she dialed the Iyohas.

'hello' she said when the line came through.

'ohh my sweet' a soft voice echoed, 'do you know....' the voice continued 'that we waited for you up till 7pm before we realize that you would not be coming'?

'am so, so, sorry ma. I did a very late shopping and when I got back, I was so tired and even forgot. Am really sorry, please Mrs. Iyoha I will make it up to you ma'.

'ok my sweet though we were worried but it was good you called'. Bisi thanked her and hung up. She further reduced the temperature of the air conditioner and closed her eyes to sleep.

When Obakpolor saw Bisi coming out of the Oba market, he heaved a sigh of relief. Ojomo was right; he had told him that the fastest way to trace Bisi was to wait for her around the Oba market vicinity since it was her favorite market. He had obeyed and had been coming every day and today he has been rewarded. He quickly started the Honda CRV and engaged gears. Obakpolor was a dark and fat usual guy, who had a reputation of tailing people. Though he had a record with the Kano state police department of a murder case, he came out clean since there was no concrete evidence to pin him to the murder scene. He licked his lips tenderly, as Bisi entered her car. Some babe he thought to himself; he followed the Rav 4 from a safe distance through the traffic into Obakhabye road and watched her pick up somebody. Obakpolor studied the girl, she was also a pretty babe; he shrugged his shoulders, his business was Bisi and not this stranger.

When Bisi dropped the stranger, he drove past and parked about a hundred feet away watching carefully from his inner mirror. When he finally got to Bisi's house, he parked some five houses away, gave her 10mins and came out of his car, it was dark now. He walked back to the flat, climbed in from the fence and watched her from the window prepare herself to sleep. When Bisi took off her clothes, Obakpolor almost jumped into the house. He dragged his eyes reluctantly from the naked body and assessed the house. He almost did not see her come to the window, he quickly ducked as she leaned out to pulled the glass in; he licked his lips tenderly as he caught a glimpse of her breast dangling out. He listened as she made her call then waited for an hour to be sure she was fast asleep.

When she fell asleep, he got into the apartment through the kitchen window that had no protector, tiptoed to the living room and searched carefully but thoroughly to see if there was any document or evidence that would link his boss. He went through all the rooms except where Bisi was sleeping, satisfied there were none, he left the flat and went back to his car. He got in and headed for his hotel. At least he had known her new house now he thought to himself that was something.

The deafening horn at the gate, jerked Bisi from the bed. She got up, wrapped herself with a wrapper under her pillow and came to the living room.

'who will that be'? she said looking at the wall clock in the living room.

'good grief'! she exclaimed, it was already past ten. The horn came again and she looked out from the window. A Mercedes Benz E 300 was outside the gate. Bisi smiled as she knew it was Ufan. She quickly collected the gate keys from the stool, opened the front door and went out to open the gate. Ufan wind the glass down and slightly brought out her head.

'nah wa for you oooo' Bisi said using her hands to push back her blonde hair. 'but you said....'

'yeh yehh,' Ufan interrupted, my boss asked me to relax this week, am even thinking about going on leave'.

Bisi open the gate and step aside for her to enter the compound. She drove straight to the car porch, parked and got out.

Ufan is of average height with a pretty face. Her hair is short and neat. She has small lips, big round eyes and a firm breast. She was wearing a stretch jean, a body hug that brought out all her endowments and a black canvas.

'so you've been sleeping ehhhh?' she said closing the car door.

'don't mind me' Bisi said locking the gate; 'you are really looking hot and take away ooo, how come no guy kidnapped you before you got here'?

Ufan laughed as Bisi led the way to the apartment.

'let me help you tidy the house up while you take your bath, now how is that?'

'you're a darling dear, thanks.' Bisi went into the bath room while Ufan got herself busy inside the kitchen. When she was through, she watched her hands, went to one of the rooms to re-do her makeup. She came to the living room and missed a whisky and soda, poured it into two short glasses and put a cracked ice in her own.

'How do I look'?

Ufan put her glass down, turn round to look at her. Bisi was putting on a black jean trousers with a white polo and blue jean jacket. She stamped the blue addidas canvas on the tiles waiting for Ufan's remarks.

'why, you know you are a pretty girl, anything you wear goes' Ufan handed Bisi her glass.

'I can see everywhere is neat, thanks'.

'ohhhh, it's nothing girl'.

'Finish your drink in time' Bisi said as she drank her own in a gulp

'why'?

'we're going out'. Ufan's eyes lighted up.

'and where exactly do you have in mind.'

'well, errh.., to somewhere lonely I guess'. Bisi picked up her car keys from the dining table, dropped her glass and went outside. Ufan emptied her drink inside her mouth, dropped it on the dining and locked the front door. She opened the gate for Bisi who drove out and waited for Ufan. She locked the gate and joined Bisi in the car and they took off.

CHAPTER THREE

Obakpolor eased gears and followed the Toyota Rav 4 that was now racing fast into the traffic. As the Rav 4 picked up speed, he had problem keeping up with it. He cursed softly as he tried to overtake the old land rover blocking him but stiffened as the Rav 4 headed for the high way. It would be easy for Bisi to know that she is being followed now. He tried to stay behind a Toyota Camry but the goat won't move fast enough, he had no other choice than to overtake it. He immediately felt naked as both of them were now alone on the high way. Obakpolor hesitated for a moment following her but what if she was headed for somewhere that will be of importance to them. He relaxed his mind and just followed, there was nothing he could do now. He would have to now rely on luck that Bisi won't know if she is being followed.

Bisi was now running 120km/hr.; she began to suspect the Honda CRV tailing her. She grimaced and increased her speed up to 150 km/h and noticed the Honda still kept a distance.

'have you gone crazy'? Ufan asked 'remember the Road Safety Corps patrol this high way.'

'I know that dear, but trust me I know what am doing'

'what's up girl, talk to me'

'we're being followed' Bisi said pointing back with her thumb.

'what makes you think so'? Ufan said looking back.

'I can swear I saw that Honda at the Oba market yesterday and when we were coming out of my street, I caught a glimpse of it.'

'I still don't get it. Why will somebody be tailing you?'

'you'll know when we are through with this goat'.

She slowed down as she saw a petrol station ahead, indicated in the pointer and swung the Rav4 into the station.

'do we do it here'? Ufan asked

'no, let's pretend to buy fuel'. As the petrol attendant attended to them, Obakpolor came into the station and pretended to buy fuel too.

'don't rush it' Bisi told the petrol attendant, fill it up slowly'.

Obakpolor pulled up by a pump, asked the fuel attendant to fill it up and wandered into the super market pulling his cap down. He wondered if they've noticed him, well he thought if they notice him, then he would have to give them some space. They seem to have been minding their business that might mean that they have not taken notice of him he thought; he watched the Rav 4 roll out quietly from the station. He had always wanted a Rav 4 but the car dealer had somehow convinced him to go for the Honda CRV; he pushed the thought away from his mind and strolled out of the super market.

'Is she full'? he asked the fuel attendant

'no sir, but it's coming up now'.

'Don't worry its ok'. He paid for the fuel and drove off.

Both girls looked back and saw the Honda some distance away. Bisi smiled and increased her speed to 120 km/h. she was sure she alone can handle him; when Obakpolor had come out of his car, she had studied him. She thanked her stars that she was having a black belt in taekwondo. Ayo had encouraged her to learn it when they started going out. He had always taken her to the Samuel Ogbemudia stadium in Benin for constant taekwondo exercises and that was where she met Ufan who was already holding a black belt before they came in. She slowed down and turned right to the Hive hotel just after the Oluku junction. Bisi drove through the gates and selected an emergency parking space. They got out pretending not to see Obakpolor driving in and made their way into the dance hall. The hall was dark but lightened with dimmed coloured disco lights; a DJ was in control and the air was charged with music and shouts of excitement by ladies inside the hall. Bisi and Ufan carefully selected two single chairs and a table separated from others where they could observe the place and sat down.

'leave him to me' Ufan said

'okkk… but please watch it oooo, these people are assassins'.

'I will girl, trust me on this one'.

Obakpolor strolled into the dancing hall feeling totaling naked and ashamed. He stood for some time trying to adjust his eyes to the dimmed lights inside the hall. Despite the crowd of dancers and the heavily charged atmosphere, he was sure his cover was blown; he would have followed his instinct, he wouldn't have followed them here in the first place he thought. He began to make his way slowly through the people to the bar as they danced widely. He asked the barman to mix an Irish whisky and a martini for him and waited. The barman nodded to him and mixed the drink; Obakpolor leaned on the bar looking round the hall casually and sighted Bisi and the friend.

'that will be three hundred naira'. The barman said;

Obakpolor turned round; he nodded and paid for the drink, took it in a gulp and returned the glass to the bartender. He then made his way back into the crowd; he looked kind of tense so he danced a little trying to look for a spot to sit. As he sighted a lone chair at the corner of the hall, about 40 yards away from the girls, he quickly made his way there and sat down. He searched his pocket, brought out a cigarette and paused to light it. As he raised his head up, he saw a girl coming towards him.

'good grief' he muttered to himself grasping for air from the smoke, 'I could lay this broad for a week and I'll still not be satisfied'. Obakpolor was carried away with the undulating figure and shape coming towards him, he did not see the look in her eyes; the cloud of smoke prevented him from noticing the rage but by the time he saw it, he was too late. Although he was quick enough to pull his gun from his holster, he was not smart enough to pull the trigger. Ufan delivered a sharp flying kick on his head. There was cracking of bones; he fell backwards crashing with the chair. He tried to raise his gun to fire it but she gathered strength and hit him again very hard on the same spot and her low but sharp heeled shoe tore his forehead open. Obakpolor, still trying to figure out what had hit him, fell into oblivion, clouds of darkness covered him. All he could hear were the shouts of excitement from the electrifying dancing hall, he saw the girl bending over him and it was darkness.

Lawani Peters sat in his office deep in thoughts. Bamidele had gone the previous evening to Togo while Alhaji had just left for Senegal. He was in charge now. His mind went back to the year they had just started their organization. He had met Alhaji in Minna after the Nigerian civil war and they had planned and formed the 'Amamadas'. Alhaji had made his money during the civil war in the country by smuggling arms into the country and selling them to the rebels. Once he was caught by the government troops but somehow he escaped, changed his name and entered his billions. He had wished the war to continue so as to make more money. When the Amamadas was six months old, Alhaji decided to open a cigarette company and a wine factory as a cover up. Through this company, he had earned his fame and made more money both within and outside the country. By the time Alhaji tried to open a mining company, he ran into issues with the change of government when the new Minister discovered the fraud in the contract agreement and his license was revoked. Despite all his political connections, it was difficult convincing the new President hence he made of his mind to cause another chaos in the country so they can be in the race for arm sales again and recoup his loss. Alhaji and Lawani knew that though five decades have passed since the Nigerian civil war, the scars of the war and taste for vengeance were still evident amongst some of the tribes though kind of suppressed. They strongly believe that once they start the crisis, they would withdraw to their bunker and begin to sell arms to the insurgents, militants and any other aggrieved tribal group that have suppressed their hatred for long.

Lawani brought his mind to Ayo Lewis, who they kidnapped because of his relevance to the success of their organization and they are totaling relying on him. As a mechanical engineer, his jobs is to make sure all their equipment, machines and vehicles are in good working condition.

'I want you to get rid of Ayo as soon as his services are over, he knows too much' Alhaji had told him.

He turned his mind to Bamidele whose sister they had kidnapped to get his attention to work for them and do some very dirty jobs for the organization. Dele and his sister too would have to be taken care of when the operation is over. He knew Dele was doing his best to make an impression but he also knows that even with the chip planted inside him, his cop instinct might make him be a bit of a problem to deal with. He pushed the thoughts away and raised the red telephone receiver;

'any message from Obakpolor yet'?

'no sir'. the female voice said. 'since he reported of Bisi's new house, we've not heard from him again.'

'very well then, have you checked his hotel'?

'no sir'

''please do' he said and hang up.

Lawani was now thinking of Bisi. Has Ayo somehow gotten a message to her, telling her about what was brewing? He struggled with the thought and finally forced himself to conclude that Bisi do not know anything. After all Ayo was under very tight security and heavily guarded. The red telephone rang and he picked it up at the first ring.

'yes'?

'sir, he is not in the hotel; the receptionist said they've not see him since the last seventeen hours.'

'okay, pack up, we are moving to Yola'

'sir do you mean Adamawa state'?

'you heard me' Lawani said trying to control his impatience. 'we are staying at the plaza de Richie in Yola, so clear up; Any other questions.'

'no sir'.

Bamidele came out of the Lome international airport and waved a Renault taxi coming towards him.

'take me to the hotel de' camp' he said in French getting into the back seat. The driver drove through the airport traffic, came out of the gates and headed for the high way.

'hey buddy,' Dele said learning forward; you are heading the wrong way'.

But the driver drove deaf mute. Bamidele reached out for his neck but it was too late as a glass came from nowhere and separated them. He checked the car doors but they were both locked. He studied the glass and saw they were fortified; he then relaxed in the seat, waiting for the worst to happen.

He was that kind of person that never fears as he always had confidence in his abilities and training. Wherever this deaf mute was taking him to, they would have to be good or else they will be sorry. He opened his brief case and quietly opened the concealed part. He brought out his Mauser and checked it, satisfied it was ok; he screwed the silencer to it. Dele rolled up his trouser, dug the gun into the elastic band on his leg and dropped the trouser. These bastards are going to get a surprise since they would not be expecting him to have brought a gun into the country through the airport.

The driver looked back causally to see Bamidele; he slowed down and turned into a lonely dusty road. The Renault raced down the road with dust trailing it behind. As it got to an open field, the driver pulled up in front of a black Volkswagen Passat car. Three men got out of the car while one was short, the other two were about 5.11' feet tall and were all dressed up in immaculate suite. The shorter one beckoned on the driver, who got out and walked towards them. Bamidele quickly surveyed the environment and searched to see if there were more somewhere, apart from the persons in front of him, they were alone. The dust was settling down and he could see the shorter one giving the driver something. The driver came back and opened the door as the three men close in. Dele came out swiftly hitting the driver very hard in his throat, it choked him and he jerked backwards falling on one of the tall men. Flying like a bat, Bamidele launched one full kick on the short man. The leg hit his head and Bamidele could hear bones cracking; the third man aimed a punch at his chest but Dele saw it coming. He ducked to the right and the punch went past him. Dele gathered weight in his left leg and hit him in his groin. The man squealed like a pig, fell forward and stretched out like a roosted suya on the dusty road. The first man had just pushed off the driver from off him and was aiming a Beretta 92 at Bamidele, moving like lighting, Dele hit the ground pulling his Mauser. Both guns went off the same time; the gunman looked at his suite, blood was coming out of the breast pockets. He looked at Dele with shock and bewilderment in his eyes then he fell forward like a dead wood. Looking around, Dele saw the driver making for the door of the taxi seriously coughing as he held on to his throat. He quickly got up and pursued him. He caught up with the taxi driver as he was opening the car door; Dele turned him round, heaved him up and slammed him hard on the bonnet of the car.

'please let me go, I have a family, please '. The man screamed.

'ohhhh, so you can talk now ehhhh'. Dele held on to his throat and applied pressure.

'please don't kill me please' the driver struggled to say his eyes turning red, and his mouth opened wide trying to grasp for air.

'are you ready to tell me what this was about'? Bamidele barked, his eyes snapped fire. The driver struggled to nod his head and Dele let him go; he fell of the bonnet coughing uncontrollably.

'good boy' Bamidele said dusting dirt off his clothes. He gave the driver space to regain his breath. The taxi driver was a fat man and was not use to such type of exercise.

'so who are these men'?

'I don't know them before. They approached me in our park; asked me to bring you here and promised to pay me well; please that's all I know I beg you.'

'so how come you know me' Dele asked quietly, watching him.

'they gave me your photo, and gave me half of the money'.

Bamidele brought out the Mauser with its cone shaped silencer and pointed it at his chest.

'who are these corpses'? he asked again ignoring all what the driver has just said.

'I tell you I don't know, please believe me'. He started crying as thick cold sweat ran down his face.

'okay, wait here'. Dele went to the men lying on the ground. The man he had shot was dead alright, his white suite covered in red. He looked passed the one he had broken his skull and the one he hit in his groins. Satisfied that all were dead, he went through their pockets; there was nothing of interest so he walked to the Passat and searched it thoroughly; there was nothing of interest there too. He walked back to the taxi and motioned the driver to get in as he got into the back seat.

'okay buddy, you can now take me to my hotel'.

CHAPTER FOUR

'You've killed him'. Bisi said running towards Ufan.

'yes, sorry I had to'.

'oohhh, you shouldn't have killed him. We would have gotten some information from him.'

'Look sister, he pulled a gun at me that was why I had to hit him so hard'.

'Ok girl, no offence taken, but let's get out of here as fast as we can.'

'Wait'! Ufan said. She looked round the hall, it was still charged up and people were still dancing going about their business. She opened Bisi's bag and searched it, there was a hand glove and handkerchief inside; she wore them, and then bent down to searched his pockets. There was nothing in his pockets except for a bunch of key and some rolls of 500 naira bills.

'come on, Ufan let's not waste time here, this place is too crowded, someone might see us'.

'go ahead Bisi, just get the car started I will be right behind you'. Bisi hurried through the hall and made her way to the car, got in and started it. Ufan quickly went to work with the gloves; she removed two bullets from the Mauser, soaked them in the blood coming out from his head and used her thumb to push the bullets deep into his brains. She straightened up and stepped back, satisfied it was a perfect job, she looked round the hall again. It was business as usual. She removed the gloves and began to press through the crowded hall. She came out in the open and entered the car.

'what have you been doing'? Bisi asked.

'ohh, I was just looking at the man that committed suicide inside the hall'. As Ufan got in Bisi shot the car immediately out of the hotel. She entered the Benin-Lagos high way and headed home.

'can you tell me exactly what this is about'?

'yes, but it's not much. Since six weeks now, I've not seen Ayo. I tried looking for him but all my efforts were fruitless. Then suddenly, three men appeared inside my bedroom in my former apartment, at about 2am. Please don't ask me how they got in cos' I don't know myself.' Ufan closed her eyes and leaned her head on the head rest.

'are you listening to me?'

'keep talking, am with you.'

'so the men took me by surprised with their blazing guns and tried to kidnapped me, but thanks to Jeg, he came to rescue me.'

'was that why you packed into a new place'?

'Yehh yehh. They were now approaching a bridge.

'pull over when you've climbed the bridge'.

'what for'? Bisi asked as she slowed the car down, she brought it to a halt and killed the engine.

'am disposing the hankie and glove. Ufan got out; she took the napkin at the back seat, tied the hankie and gloves to a block and threw the block into the river. She watched the block sink into the river and then got into the car. Bisi started the car and engaged the gear, she stepped on the pedal as Ufan entered and slammed the door.

'did you use the gloves on the corpse'?

'exactly, now if you would continue with your story......'

'were was I'?

'you were talking about packing when you stopped the car.'

'yes, so am suspecting that they kidnapped Ayo.'

'what makes you think that'?

'well I don't know, it's just a hunch. Why will three strange looking men come into my apartment, gag me on my bed; weeks after Ayo got missing?'

'why didn't you report this issue to the police?

'well, I really don't want them into it. These people might harm Ayo if I go to the police'. She slowed the car down as they approached her street. The

Rav 4 entered the street slowly and raced down the road. Bisi stopped the car in front of the gate. Ufan was already out to open it; Bisi drove in and parked as Ufan locked the gates.

'what a day' Ufan said coming up to Bisi that was now opening the front door.

'I don't know about you, but am famished.'

'you can say that again girl'. They both headed for the kitchen, Bisi brought out a full roasted chicken from the oven and carried it to the dining.

'now that's what am taking about' Ufan said. 'Let's eat then we can finish our talk'. She opened the fridge and brought out two canned Pepsi.

Alhaji Abudu arrived in Senegal at exactly 1.08pm. A Buick saloon car was waiting for him. As he came out of the arrival hall, the car drove towards him. He got into the back seat, slammed the door and relaxed.

'which hotel am I staying'? He asked the man sitting next to him.

'always the best Mr. Abudu, always the best'. The man was massively built with broad shoulders. He was about fifty-three, his hair was black and thick and his face was smooth with no sign of wrinkles

'move' he said tapping the driver's shoulders lightly and turning to Alhaji,

'we will discuss tomorrow morning by 9 o' clock. I hope you would be up then'?

'sure, that's why am here'

'very well then. I will send my driver to pick you up; that ok with you'? Alhaji nodded his head and closed his eyes.

The Buick negotiated through the traffic and pulled up in front of the Palace hotel.

'this is your room key, it's on the eight floor'

'thank you Mark, I'll see you tomorrow'. Alhaji went into the hotel, took the elevator to the eight floor and got out. He looked at the number on the key and made his way to room 309; he opened the door, got in and locked the door behind him. Alhaji looked round and smiled; the living room was well furnished. He crossed the room to the inner room; there was a big bed that could have taken five people conveniently and two Cain chairs facing it. This also looked good.

He dropped his brief case on the bed and went into the bathroom. Satisfied that the bathroom was also ok, he took off his clothes, took a cold shower and changed into a cream coloured suit with a deep red tie. He put on his cone shaped crocodile leather shoe, locked the brief case in the closet and came into the living room. He raised the telephone and dialed three digits.

'can I have a car outside? I need a driver to take me round the city'.

'yes sir, it will be arranged. Will a Peugeot 607 do'?

'that will be perfect' Alhaji said grinning. He dropped the receiver and came out of the room, locked the door and headed for the elevator.

As the taxi pulled up in front of the hotel de' camp, Bamidele got out and entered the hotel.

'Bonjur sir' the receptionist said as Bamidele approached her. Her smiles were broad and genuine. Deles nodded and return the same smiles.

'I was told to collect my room key from you'

'ohhh……. ehhhh pardon me, you are Mr. Bamidele I would suppose'?

Dele smiled and nodded again. She was a tall slim white French lady with a small round face. Her makeup was light and she was putting on a fitted trouser suit that revealed her curved hips; her firm breast was bulging out from the camisole under her suit and as she placed her hands on the marble plague separating them, Bamidele took notice of the fingers; they were well manicured. She opened the drawer and brought out a key as she handed it over to him, Dele reached out over the plague and touched her hips affectionately and she vibrated slightly.

'second floor' she said softly 'and sir please be sure you give me a notice before you do that next time, or I'll rape you'.

'ahhh….okkk, I think I'll better give you a notice later in the day'

'I will be waiting'. she smiled and stroked her blonde hair gently with her right hand revealing the manicured fingers again. Dele smiled back again, turned and walked briskly to the elevator. He got in and nodded to the operator inside.

'second floor' Dele said. They rode to the second floor and Dele got out. He looked at the number 39 and moved to the door that was just adjacent to the elevator; he unlocked the door and peered in.

'come inside' a deep French accent said. He hesitated, and then entered. There was a man sitting on the settee facing the door. He was holding a colt .38 in his hand pointing directly at him. Bamidele kept his face expressionless and dropped his bag on the settee near the door.

'am sorry, but I think am in the wrong room'.

'nnno not at all', another voice said 'please sit down'

Dele turned to see the other person coming out of the inner room. He was muscular, his face as hard as granite and his fingers looked like the claws of a deer. Bamidele brought his attention to the one holding the gun; he was a tall, slim man with small eyes. He was about twenty feet away from him, Dele sighed closed the door and sat down.

Bamidele was still playing calm though his nerves were all stretched out. Neither Alhaji nor the so called Lawani told him the trip would be like this. He had thought the job was to make the necessary arrangements and leave without any fuss.

'so if am not in the wrong room may I know exactly what is going on in my room'?

'plenty' the muscular man said. 'but first of all let's make introductions; my name is Paul and this gentle man here is Kola, and you'?

Bamidele at this point didn't need a prophet to tell him that Paul and Kola were of the same set with the people he had met when he just arrived.

'I believe you already know my name, so let's get on with it'.

'wrong' Paul said. 'we only have your photo not your name.'

'ok, my name is Omo Peters, now can I know what is happening here.'?

'of course' Paul said sitting down. 'but what about your escort'?

'I think they changed their minds so your humble servant brought me here alone'.

'alright'. Kola said putting the gun where he could reach it easy.'

'let's get down to business. We were asked to come down to Togo for the tanks. We know that's why you are also here; so it will be wise if you catch the next available flight back to Nigeria.'

'and if I don't…..'

'you'll be very sorry'.

'emmm sorry boys, I am not here for jokes like this. Am here for a purpose and am not living until I finish my mission here…...'

'don't be a fool' Paul cut in. 'you better return now that you are still healthy'.

'well', Bamidele said getting up; 'if you don't mind, I think am done with your speculative drivel, you can go now because I have other things to attend to.'

Paul looked at Kola and jerked his head to the door. Kola collected his gun, stood up and walked to the door to join Paul who was already at the door. He paused by the door and turned,

'bros, you better take our advice. Don't' think you are too smart o….…..o'.

'so long' Dele replied weaving his hand. As they left, he closed the door and drove the bolt home. He went round the suite and combed it thoroughly for any bugs. Satisfied the suite was clean; he walked to the telephone and dialed a number.

'Defense Ministry' a musical female voice said in French

'yes please can you put me on to the Minister' Bamidele said in French

'your name sir'?

'Peters, Mr. Omo Peters'. After some minutes, a croak voice came up;

'yes Mr. Peters'. Bamidele smiled, Alhaji had told him the name to use. Alhaji had made them to think that Mr. Peters was a representative of the Nigerian Defense Ministry and so the Togolese Government had agreed on the terms of contract without making enquiries.

'I just flew in, so when can we meet'?

'tonight, a car and an escort would come and pick you up by eleven-thirty. We'll start the meeting at twelve'. Dele looked at his watch- it was ten past eleven; he still had some time.

'okay, I'll be waiting'. He replaced the receiver, took of his clothes and went into the bath room to shower. When he was through, he put on an immaculate white suit, his black hippopotamus skin shoe made him look like a presidential aspirant. He locked his brief case inside the closet and buried the Mauser under the mattress. Dele checked his time which told him he had ten minutes more. He crossed the room to the first one and sat on the settee he had sat when Paul and Kola where in the room. This job was supposed to be easy, the way things are going now he would have to be extra careful and be alert throughout the time. As soon as he signs the papers, he would be gone; not a day more. He knew Paul and his friend meant the threat and so he won't be taking any chances; he would have to play along with Alhaji and Lawani until he can trace where they are holding his sister.

According to Lawani, seven trailers would be waiting to carry them across the border that would be Lawani's cup of tea then. The telephone interrupted his thought. He got up to answer it;

'hello sir', it was the receptionist down stairs; I hope you like your suite'?

'yes it's cozy but lonely without you here' Dele said. She chuckled and said;

'don't worry, I will come up later to warm it up for you. But that will be when you're back oookkk; because as at now, there are two government cars waiting for you outside'.

'thank you, I will come down as soon as I can'.

Dele dropped the receiver and came out of the room. This girl's English is very good and fluent he thought. He would have to cane her when he comes back; at least her shift would have been over by then. He rode the elevator down, nodded to the receptionist who just smiled. Dele came out of the hall into the terrace; he looked round, there were two governments' BMW X6 with tinted glasses parked. Feeling like a king, he got into the back seat of the front X6 and closed the door. The man in the front passenger seat turned and shook his hands.

'Mr. Omo Peters'?

'Yes' Dele replied. The driver shot the car out of the hotel and headed east. They had journeyed for about seven minutes when a land rover drove pass them with sporadic firing none stop, the slugs perforated the X6, shattered the glasses and leaving the driver in a pool of blood. The car that was already racing 120km/hr swerved slightly to the right, mounted the slabs and bounced back to the road again. Bamidele cursed and shouted at the other man to do something; he was not going to soil his immaculate white. The man held on to the wheel, he pulled the driver to himself with his right and then squeezed himself across the corpse into the driver's seat. Just then the escort overtook them and pursued the land rover that was now gathering speed.

'give me your gun'; Dele said holding out his hand.

'but sir I………..'

'give me your gun' Dele snarled; I've had enough for one day he thought. The man reached into his suite and pulled out a .45 caliber automatic.

'what is your name my friend' Dele asked as he collected the gun and checked it.

'Jomela'

'okay Jomela, make sure you get to that rover before your friends do.

'yes sir'. The BMW X6 leaped forward like a cheetah. They were now heading out of town and making for the high way that Bamidele was now familiar with. Paul and his friends probably have a base here he thought, well to hell with them, since is fight they want he was going to give them a full dose of it. Jomela overtook the escort car and came behind the land rover, the man at the back sit immediately opened fire; but Jomela was ready, he swung the BMW to the left and brought it to the side of the land rover. The man that has opened fire duck when he saw Bamidele taking his aim, the .45 caliber vibrated thrice; the slugs smashed the glass and dug a hole in the driver's neck. He jerked forward and his head hit the wind screen shattering it.

'slow down' Bamidele told Jomela, he applied the brakes and swerved to the other side of the road. The land rover vied into the bush, somersaulted and exploded almost immediately. Jomela stopped the car and the escort also came to a halt behind them. The three men inside quickly jumped out and covered the area.

'are you alright sir'? one of the escort asked.

'yes am fine but the driver is dead'.

'Who are they sir'? Jomela was asking; Bamidele looked at him fringing a surprise.

'that's exactly the questions I should be asking you'. He got out of the car and returned the gun to him.

'please get me out of here' he said looking at the dead driver.

'take him to the minister' Jomela instructed the two men in French ; ' I'll take care of the corpse'.

Bamidele and the two body guards got into the escort BMW X6 and drove off. The car drove into the minister's lodge and Dele got out before the female SSS could open the door. She saluted him and led him into the elevator and they rode to the third floor.

'after you sir' the lady said

'no you first my lady'; she smiled and shrugged her shoulders then led the way to a door marked 'PRIVATE'. Just like Alhaji's office Bamidele thought. The lady opened the door and stepped aside for him to enter, he passed her and entered; there were five men sitting around a big round desk.

'ahhh, welcome Mr. Peters'. one of the men said getting up. Judging from the white hairs that covered his head and cheeks, he was in his late sixties and about 5.12' feet tall. He was wearing a brown safari and a golden ring.

'come let me introduce you'. Bamidele moved towards him while the SSS lady closed the door and went back to her post.

CHAPTER FIVE

'what are we going to do now'? Ufan asked as she joined Bisi in the living room. She was lying on the sofa.

'not a thing'

'what do you mean not a thing? By my assessment, the pressure is high now and you want to still relax'?

'look girl' Bisi started sitting up; if we had found anything on the man who is now a corpse, we would have used that as a start but right now we have nothing'.

'well I don't see how we could have ever gotten any relevant information from that man. Common Bisi, we're dealing with professionals here and remember that place was public. Besides, by the time his employers get to find out, they will come all out.'

Bisi stood up and walked to the standing mirror, looked herself over and turned to Ufan.

'do you think I should change my look?'

'hhmm that's a nice one, maybe that would stall them for some time until they trace you through your office.'

' I don't think they know where I work…..'

'Ayo might have talked' Ufan interrupted her; 'besides, this people have traced you out twice now. I don't think they would be careless in their third attempt.'

'stop frightening me! Anyway, I agree with you but I don't think Ayo could have turned me over to them just like that'.

'what if we turn this matter to the police'?

'yeah, that's what I should have done'. Bisi said coming back to sit down. 'But you see Ufan, just like I told you before; I don't want them in it. If only Jegbefo was around…..'

her cell phone jotted them as it went off, Bisi reached for it on the table and picked it up.

'hello' a male voice said.

'who is it'?

'Mr. Ola'

'ohhhh good afternoon sir, am so sorry I didn't check the caller before picking'.

'It's okay' he replied.

Mr. Ola is the national chairman of the Nigerian Society of Engineers and Ayo Lewis is the secretary. Ayo had gotten a six weeks' vacation and Mr. Ola had wanted him to sign some papers before proceeding on his vacation and though Ayo had promised to sign the papers the following morning he had not showed up ever since.

'I've been trying to reach you for some time now. I've checked your former house and even your colleagues don't seem to know where you are spending your leave.'

'I..I…. I…am very sorry sir, just that I packed out without informing anyone. But how did you get my new line'?

'Nosa gave it to me yesterday'.

Okkkay, do you want anything sir'?

'yes I wanted to ask you about Ayo.' Bisi stiffened; she signaled Ufan and put the cell phone on speaker.

'what about him sir'.

'there are papers he had to sign before his leave but he had not shown up'. Bisi's mind raced, Ola needs to be kept out of this. He looked at Ufan who shook her head.

'emm am sorry sir, Ayo has long left for Hong Kong'.

'is that where he is spending his vacation'?

'yes'.

'can you give me his contact or send a message to him for me'?

'am afraid I can't sir'

'why'?

'because he is touring Asia. He doesn't have a definite address.' Bisi glanced at Ufan who nodded her approval.

'okay, please when he calls you, do get my message to him, it's very important'. Bisi told him she would do just that and sent her regards to his family.

'phew!' she exclaimed. 'that was definitely a close one'.

She looked at her palms and noticed she was sweating.

'I think we should call your detective friend to help us. I don't think we can hold on like this for long'.

'it's no good, he is out of town'.

Ufan paced to the window and gazed outside not sure what she was looking for. She searched her brains for a solution outside the police but none came. Bisi switched on the radio and relaxed her head on the sofa. Finally, Ufan raised her hands in exhaustion and turned to Bisi.

'am going to the loo'. Bisi closed her eyes as Ufan crossed the living room into the lobby. She was beginning to enjoy the jazz music when it was interrupted by a special announcement.

'the states CID have found a corpse along the Benin-Lagos road' the announcer said. Bisi sat up.

'the police' the voice continued 'believes the corpse had been dead since four days ago. A statement from the PRO of the police headquarters, said the decease had committed suicide. The corpse was later identified as Obakpolor after the police had traced him to the Bazem hotel where he had lodged before his death. The corpse has been deposited at the Central hospital morgue for his relations to come forward and claim him.'

Bisi smiled when the jazz music began to play again. So Ufan's work on the corpse had paid off she thought but wondered what took the police so long to find the corpse and how come the body was not found inside the dance hall.

'What's biting you'? Ufan asked coming into the living room. 'you seem to be smiling to yourself'.

'You're right'. Bisi said and told her about the news.

'if not for your handiwork, the police would have been looking for his killers by now.' Ufan felt a jolt of excitement run through her.

'it looks the cards are falling our way, but one wonders how come the corpse was not found in the hotel'. Ufan said

'well, maybe the hotel's PRO department would have paid not to have them mentioned, you know that can be bad for business....'.

The doorbell rang.

'I'll get it Ufan said and went to answer it. She slide the chain and open the door then went out to the gate, it was s courier boy. A few minutes later, she came back with a brown envelop.

'what is it'? Bisi asked

'search me'. She gave it to Bisi and stood in front of her with her hands in akimbo. Bisi opened it and looked inside, there were two pictures inside. She brought them out and turned into stone when she saw them clearly.

'what's wrong'? Ufan said snatching the picture from her. She stiffened as she saw herself squatting down by the side of Obakpolor searching his pockets while Bisi was watching.

The doorbell woke Alhaji Abudu up. He remained motionless for about a minute or so until the bell rang again. He rolled out of bed and glanced at his wrist watch under the pillow. It was 8am sharp. He muttered something under his breath and got up; he crossed the room to the living room and opened the door.

'good morning sir', the steward said as he rolled the trolley to the center of the room. Alhaji just nodded and closed the door.

'you've got a letter sir'

'from where'?

'from one Mr. Mark sir'. He collected the letter and told the steward to come back later. Alhaji locked the door behind him and checked the food in the trolley. There was a cup of coffee, omelets and four slices of bread. He closed it and opened the letter. It was Mr. Mark telling him to get ready on time as he would be coming himself to pick him up by nine. He looked at the time; it was 8:09am now.

'shit' he exclaimed 'I'll have to hurry'.

It took him 15mintues to wash and dress up; he quickly ate his meal and called the steward. As he sat on the sofa waiting for the telephone to ring, he felt sleepy. He cursed himself for getting back late to the hotel. Since three days he came to Senegal, he has been busy touring and waiting for Mark to convey the meeting he came for. The phone interrupted his thoughts and he picked it up at its first ring.

'There is a black Benz ML downstairs waiting for you sir'.

'Thank you'. He replaced the receiver, carried his brief case and stepped out of the room while locking it with his key. Alhaji took the elevator down, crossed the hall to the terrace and got into the back seat of the ML.

'Good morning Alhaji', Mr. Mark said

'Morning';

'Move', Mark told the driver. Alhaji took a casual look at Mark, his thick black hair, steady brown eyes and a calm expression gave him the confidence he enjoys. That was one thing about Mark; Alhaji thought, he always trusted himself.

'but you told me that you'll send your driver to pick me?'

'Yeah that was what I said, but something new is up' for a moment bewilderment showed in Alhaji's eyes but he quickly recovered himself and smiled.

'What's new Mark'? He asked

'the rest of my collogues won't play' Alhaji confident smiles faded away like the opening of a door.

'they think you won't succeed and that means that our supplies would be destroyed like toys'.

Alhaji dug his hands into his suite and brought out a cigar, lit it and pulled the smoke into his heart, his mind was busy. He gently blew the smoke out from his nostrils and turned to Mark.

'I thought you had that angle covered' he managed to say. He was already angry but he had to watch his temper if he wanted what he came for; Mark stared out of the window for a minute ignoring Alhaji.

'Well?'

'That's why I came to tell you, I just want to give you heads up'. Alhaji laughed out loud pushing his head backwards.

'So they think they can out smart me huh'? Mark turned his cold look at him.

'That's the position Alhaji, and they mean it. So you better be careful with them'.

They remained silent for the rest of the drive. The driver slowed down as they approached Hotel de Paradise. The ML entered through the back gates and squeezed itself between a Volkswagen Jetta and a fiat.

'this way Alhaji', Mark said getting out of the car. They walked into the hotel and took the elevator to the seventh floor.

'who is the Chairman of the meeting?'. Alhaji asked.

'Osundo'.

They walked down the corridor and came to the door marked 22, Mark rapped on the door lightly, opened it and stepped aside; Alhaji entered with Mark following, he closed the door carefully behind them. The room was a large conference room with a long hollow desk at the center. Six men were seated around the desk.

'well gentlemen', Mark started, sorry we are a bit late'.

'Welcome Alhaji', a man said standing up with his right hand held out. He was a tall dark man with broad shoulders; he had small eyes, fat nose and an average mouth with clean set of white teeth which added colour to his smiles. From the dimples and wrinkles on his face, he would be around sixty-six or so.

'hello' Mr. Touboa'. Alhaji said taking his hand. 'I hope all is well with you'.

'Ohhh sure'. Touboa chuckled.

'this is Mr. Joshua' Mark said pointing to a slim tall man with white hairs. He wore traditional attire and a cap to match. He looked sternly at Alhaji and nodded his head.

'And the next man to Joshua' Mark continued 'is Mr. Osundo'. Osundo was too busy playing with the ring on his finger to notice Alhaji staring at him. Please the rest will not like to be introduced.

'that's okay with me' Alhaji said sitting next to Touboa.

They had known way back before the Nigerian civil war and were in the business of selling arms and ammunitions to rebels. While Alhaji had established a cigarette company in Nigeria, Touboa had opened up a beverage and juice factory in Togo. And both of them had also been fingered in the news of arms trade in the Angola, Liberian and Sierra-Leone war though they denied it.

'I think is high time we start this meeting one of the un-introduced men snapped.

'Alright,' Alhaji started putting his briefcase on the desk. 'You all know why am here but let me address you formally. My organization is about to overthrow my country's present government and am here to seek help from you.'

'what kind of help are you talking about?' Osundo asked removing his ring from his hand. Alhaji took in a deep breath, brought out a list from his briefcase and put it on the table.

'I will need 2 jetfighters, 2 submarines along with ammunitions, military trucks; it's all on the list'. He pushed the list to Mark, who began distributing copies to all.

'I think what you are asking for is way too much for us to let you have'. One of the un-introduced men said, without even looking at the list; his eyes snapped fire.

'Well if you are thinking of the money...............'

'he is not thinking about the money Alhaji' Touboa said

'Alhaji, I think you are crazy to ever imagine overthrowing the Nigerian government'. Osundo started. 'have you forgotten the Nigerian civil war in a hurry? Have you thought about the socio-economic situation it would create across the sub-Saharan, refugee crisis......?'

'please don't teach me war lessons' Alhaji interrupted

'but the bottom line is that you can't win'? Osundo insisted.

'and why do you think so'? Alhaji queried.

"He thinks so because your country is too strong for you to attempt what you are planning'. Touboa said.

'Now you guys listen, I didn't come here to hear war lessons and discouragement. For heaven's sake just tell me if you are going to do business with me on this or not.'

Alhaji was now having difficulty controlling his anger. He put his two palms on the desk and rapped on it.

'okay, Alhaji' Osundo started,' you are playing with dynamite and you don't seems to know it. You don't seem to care what the international community would do; but we will give you what we can release provided our name is not mentioned when the plan goes sour'.

'of course your name is out of this. I have my own strategy for this operation; and so mark my words, it will not turn sour'.

The seven men began speaking French and a heated argument ensured. Alhaji watched them as they argued with frayed nerves and closed his eyes. He had really relied on this to work as it would be very difficult to get an organization like this with such resources within the sub Saharan Africa continent.

'Okay Alhaji' Osundo said, 'we can only give you 2 jetfighters, 1 sub, 20 military trucks loaded with ammunitions but no men.'

'Hey!' Alhaji cried out, but that's not fair, where do I get the men to man the machines and equipment?'

'You will have to look for' Touboa said. 'Our boys lives are very precious to us'.

'what about the artilleries? Are you not giving me that?'

Osundo stood up and walked to a safe behind a portrait picture and came back with some documents.

"Alhaji' he said, 'you will please excuse us now.' Alhaji looked at Mark who nodded his head. He got up slowly and went out. After another round of heated deliberations that seems like a decade to Alhaji, he was called in to sign some of the papers.

'well?', he said seating down.

'we are sorry that's the only way we can help' Touboa said

'Listen to me' Alhaji said

'No you listen' One of the un-introduced man said cutting Alhaji short.

'You are planning to cause a civil war in your country, which seem impossible because the strength of your country is too much for you. And we are very sure that even if we give you everything you asked for, you will definitely come back for more. Besides, a source said you'll soon be bankrupt, so doing business with you is even a very risky business right now'

Alhaji face was as white as a bone. Though he was warned by Mark, he had not thought the meeting would go this way. He moved uneasily on his chair. No one had ever hit him so hard like this. How the hell did they even know he was having financial problems he asked himself.

'Well Alhaji', Osundo said 'Are you going to do business or not?' Alhaji looked at Mark who forced himself to meet his eyes.

'Okay, I will take them' his voice a croak. They sorted out the money and arrival date and Alhaji signed the papers. He got up thanked them and made for the door. When he got to the door, he paused and asked

'How do I get to my hotel?' 'My driver is waiting for you downstairs' Mark said. Alhaji went out of the room and rode the elevator down, crossed the reception and saw the car waiting at the entrance to the hotel. He got in and the car zoomed off. It took them seven meetings to get back to the hotel.

'Wait here' he told the driver as he stepped out of the car. He took the elevator up to his suite and packed his things up. He moved to the front door, paused and looked back, satisfied that he had not forgotten anything, he went out.

CHAPTER SIX

The Arik Air Boeing 747 plane touched down in Kano international airport. The plane raced through the runway for sometimes and came to a halt with squeal of brakes. As the door of the plane opened, Bamidele was the first to step out. He quickly made his way through the arrival hall after passing through the customs and immigration officials.

Lawani was there waiting for him. He got up sighting Bamidele and waved him.

'how was your trip?' Lawani asked taking Dele's hand

'fine'; Bamidele said surprised Lawani came to the airport himself.

They made their way to a brown Land rover and got in. the driver started the car and slowly brought the car out of the airport.

'have you packed to Yola?'

'yes'.

Bamidele relaxed in the seat.

'well, I guess that's where we ought to be right?'

'yes'. Lawani said again. He was not in the mood of talking. They both remained silent until the driver swung the SUV into a narrow path. He slowed down as they approached a waiting helicopter. They quickly got out of the car, climbed in and the chopper took off immediately. Bamidele looked out from the window and saw the Land rover going back to the main road. Sixty-two minutes later, the chopper touched on the landing pad on the roof of the plaza hotel in Yola. They both got out and took the elevator down to the tenth floor.

'welcome sir' Lawani 's secretary said. She was a tall slim girl with small breast. Her hips were slightly curved and her bow legs locked up in a black leather shoe. Her skirt and blouse was designed after the Hausa attire.

'thank you' Lawani said leading Bamidele into his office. Bamidele sat down in one of the chairs and relaxed.

'well? How far did you go?'

Bamidele told Lawani in details all what happened in Togo and concluded that he had signed the agreement with the Togolese government'.

'when are the tanks coming in?'

'tonight'. Lawani beamed.

'are you sure no one followed you?'

'I missed my first flight before I convinced myself that I was not being followed'.

'okay' Lawani said smiling. He picked up the red telephone receiver and dialed a number, after a few moments the line came through.

'yes' a deep rich voice said at the other end of the line

'hello chief, its Lawani '.

'do you have anything for me?'

'sure the package would be coming in tonight'

'from which part of the country?'

'kwara'

'okay' the chief said, 'I will tell the boys but what is the exact time'.

Lawani looked up at Bamidele who was now nursing a bottle of whisky.

'when are the tanks coming in?'.

'1.00am'. He replied

'1.00am' Lawani said into the mouth piece.

'that's okay with me. But how do you get them through the streets?

'that's no problem, we have seven heavy duty trailers on standby'.

'that is good thinking Lawani '.

'so chief we will expect you to be here as from 12 midnight?'. The chief said he will be there and hung up.

Lawani looked at the wall clock in his office that told him it was past 5 in the evening.

'well'? Bamidele asked putting the whisky away.

'the chief will join us by 12 midnight'. Lawani leaned forward and poured himself a drink. Just then a tap came on the door.

'come in' Lawani said. The secretary opened the door and entered. Her white face stirred up Lawani.

'what is eating you Ngozie?' he snapped. 'you look as if you swallowed a bone or something.'

His voice gave Bamidele a jolt. Slowly, he looked back and saw Ngozie standing by the door with a newspaper in her hand.

'am afraid I have bad news sir'. Lawani took a sip from his drink.

'what is it about?' he asked. Ngozie came forward, dropped the paper on the desk and moved backwards. Lawani dropped his whisky and took the paper. He read the headline- **'man commits suicide'** and stiffened when he saw photograph of Obakpolor's corpse under the headline. Bamidele saw the look on Lawani's face so he got up and took the paper from Lawani and looked at the photo. He raised his eyebrows and dropped the paper on the desk. Lawani quickly recovered from the shock and emptied the whisky into his mouth.

He took back the paper and read it in details. The room was silent as he read it while Ngozie went back to her desk. Few minutes later, Lawani dropped the newspaper on the desk; he poured another drink into his glass and took it in a gulp.

'how did they say it happen?' Bamidele asked leaning forward.

'the police said he committed suicide. He has being dead for four days before he was discovered by the police'.

'hmm I think I smell a rat. There's no way Obakpolor could have done that'.

'Obakpolor was one of our very good solider'. Lawani said pouring himself another whisky.

'I agree with you. I think he got too close to that Bisi girl and got himself killed.'

'yes I agree with you too. But I think he would have been too smart for her except she is getting help.' Lawani pressed the intercom.

'did he give you Bisi's new address?'

'No sir'.

'how was he when he spoke to you last?'

'He was fine and normal'

'okay'. Lawani cut the line, and looked at Bamidele;

'I think we are not making any progress with this Bisi of a girl'. Bamidele lit a cigar and blew a thin smoke towards Lawani.

'I think your pressure on her has to be relaxed before it escalates into something else.'

'you're are absolutely right. Now am thinking of Alhaji's response, he had already told me to leave her alone and face other serious matters'.

'well from where you stand it is not looking good since he will make the fourth man you are losing . Its time you tread more carefully, Bisi is keg of gun powder.

'well, that will be for Alhaji to decide now'.

'so you just need to tell him to thread more cautiously'.

Lawani ignored Bamidele and got up. He strolled to the window and stared at the view outside.

'there's nothing we can do now. But there is something you do not know.' Lawani came back to his chair and sat down.

'Alhaji thinks Bisi would be afraid to go to the police because we might hurt Ayo. I think by now she would know that Ayo was kidnapped.

Bisi was the first to recover from the shock of the picture. She went into the kitchen and came back with a bottle of brandy, a soda and two glasses. She mixed the drinks and handed Ufan a glass. Ufan who was now recovering from the shock took the drink and emptied the content into her mouth in a gulp. Bisi took the photographs and examined them again. She still could not understand how the pictures were taken.

'what do we do now?' Ufan found herself saying.

'search me' Bisi said. 'I honestly don't have a clue. But it's clear that someone is trying to blackmail us'.

'whoever this person is, must be very smart and has kind of caged us. We need to think up something very fast'.

Bisi searched her brains for what seems like eternity and shook her head.

'there is nothing we can do'; she finally said. 'we will need to wait for the punk and see how things turn up'.

Ufan picked up the pictures again and stared at them. Bisi was right she thought; there is really nothing they can do now. The pictures captured a full view of herself bending down by Obakpolor's corpse while Bisi stood watching. They would have to come to a sort of compromise with the blackmailer because there was no other way out.

'okay' Ufan said dropping the pictures on the table whoever the blackmailer is, must have a blind spot somehow'.

'what was that?' Bisi said turning her attention to Ufan.

'I mean we might not be the first people this punk is blackmailing; he might have done it to other persons before'.

'so?' where does that leave us?'

'look Bisi, this punks name is Emeka, it's on the photograph'.

'how do you know that?' Bisi asked picking up the photo. She glanced at the back of the photo and saw the name printed on it.

'well that does not lead us anywhere, for crying out loud there are thousands of Emeka in this country'.

'listen to me' Ufan began, leaning forward. 'by the time this man comes, he will be demanding for money and trust me, he will keep coming for more until he has drained us like a conduit pipe. We can't just sit and do nothing, we need to dig deep into him and see if he stinks…'

'and if he stinks' Bisi cuts in, 'we will have him in a bag. Good girl'

Ufan beamed with satisfaction of what she just fashioned out. 'all we have to do is pretend we have been hit'. she said.

Few minutes later the gate bell rang. Ufan got up to answer it. she opened the window blinds slightly and saw a middle age man standing by the gate.

'yes' she called out.

'Mr. Emeka please' the man called back. She looked back at Bisi and said 'our man is here girl'. She opened the door, went to the gate to open it and led him quietly back to the house.

Emeka was a hefty man with ugly facial markings. Although his tropical green suit, red tie and bowler hat made him looked like a senator, his face gave him away as a good look at him will show that he was a killer. Ufan led him to the living room and winked at Bisi as she sat with her.

'please sit down' Bisi said

'thank you'. He sat down on the sofa directly opposite them, removed his bowler hat, took a quick survey of the room and relaxed.

'nice place you have here'

'thank you' Ufan replied.

'oh please, pardon my manners, my name is Philip Emeka and am a business man based in Lagos'.

'well, I can't say it's nice to meet you' Bisi replied 'please let get straight to what brought you here'.

For a moment Emeka stared at the two girls then laughed out so loud the girls were embarrassed.

'not so fast girls, I don't like being rushed over serious matters like this. Now first of all, I will like to have a bottle of scotch to keep me going'. Bisi hesitated for a moment then got up. She came back with the scotch and a glass.

'that's my girl' he served himself, took a sip causally and sat up.

'okay girls, here is my story, I happened to be in the hotel the day you people killed that man. As a matter of fact, I love watching pretty girls; so when you two came in and went through the crowd to a vantage spot, I became more interested in the two of you. Then few minutes later, this man comes in, makes a little dumb drama at the bar and the dance floor. But I noticed he was more interested in you two than the lot; then next thing, he took a sit and seems to be watching you two so I paid more attention.'

He gulped the drink and poured himself another round.

'so when I saw you' Emeka continued pointing at Ufan. 'walking towards this gentleman, I sense there was trouble so I quickly brought out my Samsung galaxy cell to help myself.' He raised his glass towards them and drank the alcohol quietly. He set the glass down on the glass stool by the sofa and poured out another drink.

'but you girls didn't finish the job. You shouldn't have left him in such a public place like that; so I took the risk of carrying the corpse to the side of the road behind some grasses, you should have seen my clothes.......'

'look Mr. Emeka' Bisi interrupted 'we know the rest of the story. Just go straight to the point'.

'am so sorry girls, but I thought you should hear my own side of the adventure. As for the money, I would have collected twenty million naira but the man that developed the prints for me is driving me nuts. He wants me to pay him twenty million naira for him to be deaf and dumb about this whole thing'.

Both girls kept their faces expressionless as they watched him keenly. Emeka gulped the alcohol; he poured himself the fourth round of alcohol and belched quietly, he was waiting for his narration to sink properly.

'are you asking us for forty million naira?' Ufan asked jerking her head to one side.

'look girls, I would have collected something smaller if not for this ambitious fellow. He said he will turn the prints to the police if I fail to pay him the amount.'

'okay' Bisi began 'but where do you expect us to get such money from?'

Emeka grinned and sipped his drink watching the girls. He set the glass down and said.

'look girls, let's not play that game. Am very good at it, do you people think I have been folding my hands these few days? I know both of you are in money so please quit the act'.

'we are sorry but we don't' understand what you are saying'. Ufan said

'okay, if that's how you want to play it. I know you are a structural engineer' he said pointing to Bisi, 'you designed and executed the general hospital and several other major contracts in this country. While your friend here is a petroleum engineer working with the biggest oil firm in the country. She has also been involved in contracts but I can't be specific on that'.

He took few sips of his scotch and set the glass down again.

'so you see' he continued, 'the money would not be a problem to come out; by my calculation, am even generous. And please I'll collect it in dollars.'

Bola and Bisi looked at each other; they knew they have been hit. This Emeka was no push over neither was he an amateur criminal. They will have to be careful the way they handle him.

'okay' Ufan said 'how are we sure you will not come back asking for another?'

'well you have nothing to fear. As soon as you two hand over the money, I will give you the pictures and memory card if you wish then we can then go our separate ways.'

'how do we know you won't keep some to yourself?' Bisi asked.

'no' Emeka said shaking his head. 'trust me, I will stand by my word.'

'okay then, when do you want the money" Bisi asked

'I will come down here on Sunday, is that okay with you?'

'sure' both girls said simultaneously.

'but let me warn you' Emeka said dangling his fingers, 'no police or any other security operatives must hear this matter or else this pictures will be on the front pages of the Nigerian dailies. It's up to you two.'

Both girls kept quiet and kept their face expressionless. Emeka looked at them, gulped the last content and got up.

'I'll better be going if there is no more questions'. Bisi led him outside and when he had passed the gate, she locked it and came back inside. Ufan was drinking directly from the scotch bottle with her legs crossed.

'wooo wwooo Ufan, what are doing?'

'Emeka has gotten us in a bag for now. But we need to move fast before Sunday'.

'okay but you need to stop this new drinking habit hmmm…. I think there is one person that can help us out of this jam'.

Ufan got up and walked to the window with the bottle in her hand.

'and who do you have in mind?' she asked staring at the view outside. Bisi grinned.

'it's Mr. Latif, the chief of police in the state.' Bisi had never thought she would run back to Latif for help. The last time they met, the chief had promised her protection if only she would accept. Right now it was clear that Latif was her last hope. She either go for help or face Emeka alone, oh how she wished Jeg was around.

'if you think the chief will help' Ufan interrupted her thinking, 'we better see him now'. She took a sip from the bottle again.

'of course he would help but please can you stop this drinking? You will need a clear head to reason things out; besides we will need to keep the dead out'.

'how do you mean'? Ufan asked coming to rest by the settee. 'if we keep the corpse out' she continued 'how can he help us'?

'look Ufan, all we need from the chief is information that will put Emeka out of business and I trust the chief will give us such if he has any; If we tell him we are responsible for the corpse then he would want to hear the rest of the story'.

'okkay girl, got you. Am with you all the way'

'Now you are talking girl'. Bisi said collecting the bottle from her.

CHAPTER SEVEN

Alhaji Abudu sat down behind his desk burning with fury. He reflected on how the Senegalese has disappointed him, now Lawani was making issues worst after he broke the news of Obakpolor's death.

'what do you mean he is dead'? Alhaji snarled at Lawani.

'what were you thinking when you sent him after her'? He stood up in annoyance and pace up and down the office.

'must we lose our men before we attack, what is wrong with you'?

'Alhaji look at it this way....'

'no you look at it this way, I specifically told you to leave that girl alone. Was that too difficult to ask from you'?

Alhaji was red with fury; he came to lean on the desk to face Lawani.

'if you've listened to me' Alhaji continued trying hard to speak softly, 'Obakpolor would not be dead. Now I know we've not be making progress with this girl but am telling you again, please just leave that girl alone and this time I mean it'.

That was true, when Alhaji says he mean something, he meant it. As Lawani pondered on Alhaji's outburst, he grew more annoyed of Bisi. How come such a girl has become an issue of debate? There was nothing he will say now that can change Alhaji's mind. Bisi has defeated him twice and as an ex- military general, he hates defeat.

'okay Alhaji,' Lawani said sitting up, 'I will leave her for now but when I get her, I will make her beg to die'.

'just be patient Lawani , her time will come; I don't want some girl messing up this plan of ours, please'. Alhaji went round the desk and sat down on his chair and briefly told him what happened in Senegal.

'those beast', Lawani muttered under his breath, we will show them when this whole thing is over'.

Just then a tap came on the door. From the CCTV camera, Alhaji could see Bamidele. He released the door from the button on his desk and the door swung open. Bamidele stepped in as the door closed behind him. He crossed the deluxe office, nodded to Lawani and came to rest by one of the seats.

'they said you sent for me'?

'yes' Alhaji said, 'sit down'. Alhaji pushed a pack of cigar to Dele as he sat down. Dele selected one and lit it, he pulled the smoke through his mouth and released the nicotine from his nostrils.

'okay Alhaji, am all ears'.

'good, I called you for two reasons. First my meeting in Senegal did not yield much and the other is to seek your opinion on the way forward'. Alhaji dropped a list of the expected items from Senegal on the desk were Bamidele can reach it.

Bamidele leaned forward, collected the list and crushed his cigar on the ash tray. He studied it for some time and cleared his voice

'well, I have a lot to say but I'll sum it up this way. Without military trucks, you will be fighting a battle you cannot win or finish. I went through the stockpile in the ware house as you instructed yesterday and saw that things are not still ready.'

'are you suggesting we shift the day of attack'? Alhaji queried.

'am really sorry but ..I...I...I think that will be the best thing to do right now.'

'he's right Alhaji,' Lawani said with a crack voice.

'from my records, we now have four f16 jetfighters, two warship, thirty armored tanks, about four hundred surface to air and guided missiles, 55 stinger missiles and ammunitions that might not last two months.'

Lawani paused for some time and continued.

'though we have some troops on ground, we need to look at the possibility of being exposed and attacked from all these sides once we launch our offensive'.

Alhaji opened his drawer and brought out a bottle of Irish whiskey and two glasses. He placed them on the table and turned to Bamidele;

'help yourself' he said. He brought out a gold box and carefully selected a homemade cigar from inside, lit it and smoked quietly. He thought about what Dele and Lawani had said. They are right he thought; it was very obvious they were not ready. He would be deceiving himself if he thought they we ready. Even if he ordered the attack now, the boys would not be ready and they would be fighting a senseless war without enough arms to sell. He didn't want to start a war that would benefit other arms dealer than himself so there was need to plan well. He looked at Bamidele who was nursing the Irish whiskey, he is brave and he was thinking of a way to win him to his side or eliminate him completely when the time comes. He turned his attention to Lawani who was deep in thought, he was also a brave and daring solider and without him, he would not have come this far. As he thought the issue through, he searched his brains for solutions and finally he said;

'here's what we're going to do, Lawani , you will go to Lagos and meet an organization smuggling arms and ammunitions into the country; buy as many as you can. As for you Bamidele,'

Alhaji said dangling a finger at him;

'you will go to Bamako. You are going to meet the organization that tried to distract you at Lome and get us at least thirty military trucks loaded with arms.

Alhaji looked at the burning cigar in his hand and smoked it. He released the smoke and continued.

'I want to be the first selling arms to fractional war lords before competitors flood the market. We'll regroup here in three days; any questions?'

'when do we leave' Lawani asked'

'now'.

'ehhh, I think you guys are not looking at an issue yet?'

'what's that Dele' Alhaji asked

'who is handling the jets, in terms of maintenance; I hope you know Ayo can't handle that area?'

'that's no problem' Lawani said getting up. He drank his whiskey in a gulp and set the glass on the table.

've' already taken care of that' he said.

'how?' Bamidele asked

'well I tried persuading Ayo to give us a name but he refused so I made inquiries and got a friend of his. The boys are picking him up as we speak now.'

'what's his name' Bamidele asked causally.

'Nosa Obasogie, he is an aeronautic engineer'.

Bamidele cringed but managed to smile. Things were getting worse for him he thought. He poured himself a drink and took it immediately.

Nosa Obasogie was a slim young man of about 5.11' feet tall. He should be about thirty-four years of age. As an aeronautic engineer, he had good reputation and was a team player at work.

As he parked his car in front of the Nigerian Union of scientist building, he thought how he was going to spend his vacation. Ayo had told him he was going to spend his in China but he was worried that Ayo had not called him since then. As he got out of his car and walked into the secretariat, he wondered what sort of enjoyment Ayo was into that he had not called him or Bisi. He had persuaded Ufan to come with him but she had said that she wanted to be with Bisi and that he understood. He shook the thought out of his mind, entered the office and signed the necessary papers. He came out of the building and looked round.

'china' he said to himself, 'here I come'.

Without looking at the back seat, he got in and backed the door. He stiffened as he felt a cold steel at the back of his neck. He quickly glanced at the inner mirror and saw a .45 automatic pointing at him.

'move' a deep croak voice said. Without hesitation, he thumbed the starter and engaged gears.

'where are we going'? he said, his voice steady.

'just shut your trap and head for the high way' the voice said. Nosa wondered what was happening as he drove out of the premises and headed towards the high way. His mind began to race fast;

'could you please tell me what this is all about'? he snarled.

'take the next turn'

As Nosa slowed down and entered a dirty and dusty road, tick sweat broke from his face. Was this the way Ayo passed when he didn't hear from him he thought. Was he going to die? How will Ufan feel when she or his family can't find him. He raced the car down the road; well he thought whoever these suckers are will surely not get him so cheap.

'stop the car'. the voice interrupted his thought. Nosa did as he was told and relaxed in the seat. The back door opened and a heavily built man with brown suit stepped out. His face was ugly, his lips were large and his nose a little bit compressed, probably from a fight and his hair weaved backward.

'step out from the car' he snapped coming to stand very close to the front door. It was now or never Nosa thought as he opened the door and came out. As Nosa saw the man relaxed with the gun, it gave him the courage to do what he did. Nosa shot him a punch with all his weight behind it; although the man expected him to launch an attack, he hadn't expected a fast one like that. The punch arrived on his jaw which sent him off balance and he landed on the ground. Without thinking, Nosa sprang on him on the ground only to receive a kick on his abdomen. His enemy mumbled a curse; got up and launched a left handed punch at Nosa but he saw it coming. Nosa docked to the right, grabbed the hand and pulled him forward sending him into the air to land face first. The man landed with his face and broke his neck; Nosa straighten his French suit and walked slowly to him. As he knelt down beside the corpse, something hit his head from behind; as he fell, he turn to look back and he thought he saw the butt of a gun through the ray of the sun but he was too dazed to be sure. In the darkness surrounding him, stars gathered in his eyes. His head became very heavy and he could not open his eyes but when he forced them to open, the stars were still visible and he could faintly see a female figure stroking his head affectionately and telling him he was fine. He thought it was Ufan but he was not sure; Nosa closed his eyes again and there was darkness.

'yes girls'! chief Latif said to the two girls sitting opposite him.

'what can I do for you'

'weeeellll, sir' Bisi stammered 'you remember telling me to come see you whenever I need anything?'

Chief Latif nodded his head and studied her carefully.

'well, my friend and I came across this fellow in the shopping mall and he was asking for some financial assistant.'

'why was he asking you for money'? Latif queried.

'can't really say, but he said something about being wanted by the police and was trying to get out of the country.'

'so, did you give him the money'

'oh nnoo he just ran off like that. He was kind of acting weird. So we came to ask you who it might be?'

Latif looked at the girls for some time; there was a stare of doubt in his eyes. He was sure Bisi was lying but he decided to play along.

'where did you say you saw this person?'

'in mama v shopping mall' Ufan answered.

The office was quite; the chief looked at them again and opened his drawer.

'look girls, I don't know what you are playing at but most of the criminals we are looking for have either gone underground or are no more in the country.'

'trust me sir, am not framing anything up'. Latif brought out a file and dropped it on his desk.

'have not said so' Latif said with a smile.

'can you girls give a description at least?'

'off course' Bisi said. 'he is a big guy with two straight marks on his cheeks probably gotten through tribal or a fight with an appearance of a senator.'

The chief who was going through the file looked up. The look in his eyes chilled the girls.

'are you sure that was the man you saw?'

Bisi nodded her head. She caught the attention in the eyes of the police chief and she wasn't sure if this would lead to a problem of probity. The chief looked at them again, he then went through the file and brought out a picture; Ufan's heart was beating now.

'is that him?' he asked raising the picture. Seeing Emeka staring at them, both girls almost jumped to take the picture from the chief but they managed to control their selves. A jolt of excitement ran through them but they remained calm.

'yes that's him' Ufan found herself saying.

'did he give you his name'?

'no chief, he didn't.'

Latif became serious as he leaned forward and pointed at the picture.

'this man you see hear is one of the highest paid assassin on the African continent. We found out that he took custody of his boss daughter before letting her go again but his boss does not know yet'.

'how's that'?, Bisi said, 'I mean how come the boss does not know'?

The chief studied Bisi for a while again and said;

'the girl does not leave with the father cos' his based in east Africa and has not been in Nigeria for the past eight months.'

'if he knows what will happen to Emeka'? Bisi asked. Chief Latif chuckled and relaxed back in his seat.

'look girls, you don't know a thing. That man runs one of the biggest criminal organizations in the whole of Africa and he has agents everywhere in the world. Emeka is a walking corpse girls.'

'does Emeka know this'? Ufan asked trying to sound causal.

'off course he knows, that's why he needs money to buy some of the agents. Though he has long returned the girl, he would still be punished.'

Bisi and Ufan couldn't help laughing. They had Emeka by the balls now. When they break the news to him they will watch him turn to stone.

'what's the excitement for?' Latif asked

'nothing chief' Bisi replied

'but since you people want him, why not inform the boss?'

'nnnnooo' Latif said shaking his head. 'we don't work that way'.

'how so'? Ufan asked.

'we need him to identify others for us and if possible help us put Dr. Okor, his boss out of business; if they get to him before we do, he won't last a second that's why we want him first.'

This was going to be a big shocker for Emeka the girls thought. Before the girls left, the chief of police assured Bisi of police protection whenever she wants it and he led them out.

As the girls left his office, he came back to his desk, raised the red telephone receiver and dialed.

'yes chief'?

'put a man on those two girls that just left here' the chief said.

'okay sir'.

The chief dropped the receiver and went to the window; he tucked his hands deep into his pockets and watched the ladies drive out of the station.

CHAPTER EIGHT

In the Togolese capital, three government high rank officers of the country sat round a square table waiting for two other persons to join them.

'come in' one of the men said when a tap came on the door. A short fat man opened the door and stepped back.

'they are waiting for you people' he said to the men behind him. The men came in and went straight to the middle of the room.

'welcome my good friend a fat tall man said with in French.

'my name is Mr. Clifo while the other two gentlemen are Mr. Chume and Dr. Chandler and you....'

my name is Paul and this is Kola'.

'good' Clifo said. 'now we can talk'. Paul and Kola sat down and looked causally at the three men.

'well gentlemen' Paul started, how far have you gone with them?'

'nothing concrete yet' Chandler was saying.' but we are still trying to trace Omo peters; if we can't get him then we would have to report the issue to the Nigerian government'.

'doesn't seem that you guys will make any progress' kola said smiling.

'now let's appraise the situation, some organization came out from Nigeria, tricked you and got away with your tanks without any exchange and you want us to find them for you, am I right'?

'yes you are' Chume said

'so, what's in it for us'? Paul asked opening his hands wide enough to hug a girl. Clifo rubbed his hands together and placed them on the table 'don't worry about that, my government has made provision for that' he stated, Paul beamed with joy.

'and what have you made provision of if I may ask'? Clifo brought out a brief case, put it on the table and opened it. Paul took a peep at the content.

'there is a quarter of a million dollars set aside for you but first give us what we want' Clifo said.

'very well then, the organization has moved to Yola state. Our source says that they are staying in the Plaza hotel in Yola.'

Chandler rubbed his jaw, and asked

'what about names'?

'sorry we don't have that. This people are very good. That's all we know about them presently'.

'okay', clifo said closing the brief case. He stood up and handled it to Paul.

'I think we can rely on you people. If we need you, we let you know'. Paul took the brief case; they all shook hands and clifo saw them to the door. By the time he was coming back, his face had changed.

' okay guys, what do we do'? he asked

'let's turn our secret agents on them' chume said

'I agree with you Chume'; Chandler was saying 'but let's also make sure the Chadian government wipe out people like Paul and Kola. They all look the same to me'.

'okay, but what if this organization is too smart for us to get'? Clifo asked

'then we report to the Nigerian government immediately.' Chume said 'I believe they are planning on something big in the country, something to stir up trouble'.

'well, you might be right' Chandler said, 'but don't you.......' The telephone interrupted him. Clifo motioned him to answer it; he leaned forward and raised the receiver.

'yes'?

'sir, have you finished the meeting we are still on standby'?

'okay, listen, send your boys to the plaza hotel in Yola state, Nigeria. You must be careful cos' we are dealing with a highly organized group'.

'yes sir, but when do we leave sir'?

'right now' Chandler barked into the mouth piece.

'and make sure there is result or I will have your head'. The voice at the other end muttered something about not disappointing him and chandler slammed down the receiver.

'let's hope they don't flop this one' he said

Ayo Lewis was a young man in his mid-thirties. He was about six feet tall with an average muscular built. His light completion and handsome face made him distinct even inside a crowd. When he walked, he moved as if he is floating though he tries to keep his shoulders straight.

He wondered round the living room which was well furnished by Lawani. He finally came to sit on a sofa poured himself a drink that was on the table and relaxed. For the past three weeks, he had been kidnapped and kept inside this underground warehouse. He had been planning a way of escape but none seems to have worked. Every morning a guard would come and escort him to a large hall where all sorts of military equipment and weapons were stacked neatly like a large library filled with books. His primary assignments were to ensure every arsenal is in good condition. After working for about five hours, he was returned back to his room till the following morning. This had been his routine and it was killing him. The thoughts of Bisi never left his mind throughout the day and in the night. What has happened to her he wondered, has Lawani killed her, what exactly would she be doing now? But there was no answer to them. Ayo had lost his parents when he was small and he was the only surviving child. His brilliance attracted the government to him who gave him scholarship throughout his military education. But somehow he and three others had opted out for a civil live style when they came back from the UN peace keeping mission in the then war turned Liberia. He thought about the one thousand dollars Lawani promised paying into his account per day, he thought about the constant supply of good food and drinks.

'rubbish' he said aloud. He was sure these people will kill him when they are through with him; he knew the payment of a thousand dollars is a huge lie from the pit of hell. He had tried to bewitch the guard to win him over but that didn't work out too; the guard must be well paid. The rap on the door interrupted his thought. Before he could get the door, it opened and Nosa stepped in closing the door behind him. Ayo reeled back on his chair, blood left his face, and his mouth sagged open.

'where in heaven's name did you come out from'?

Nosa forced himself to smile but when the smile came, it was a grimace.

'I was helped down here' he managed to say.

'how is that?' Ayo said his voice a whisper. Nosa quickly told him his experience and how he found himself in a room next to Ayo.

'when was this'?

'two days ago I guess'

'you mean you have been in the next room for two days now'?

'yeh, until this morning when they told me I will be meeting a friend and here you are'.

'so how was Bisi and Ufan doing when you last saw them'?

'my guy, every one of them are seriously worried'. Nosa quickly made sign to ask if the room was bugged.

'noooo' Ayo said 'I guess they feel this place is a dead end for me'

'well we'll show them we are no mugs boy'

'and how are you planning on doing that'?

'don't worry, we'll find a way out'

'ahhh get that out of your chest guy' Ayo was saying, 've tried my best to get off. The only option is suicidal'.

Nosa got up and went round the room, he examined everywhere and finally shook his head.

'I think you might be right boy; the place is sealed up'.

They heard a light tap and the door opened slowly. Alhaji Abudu entered the room and left the door ajar.

'good evening gents' he said. Nosa turned but they both kept quiet.

'please sit down' Alhaji said to Nosa as he pulled a plastic chair for himself and sat were he could see both of them. Nosa hesitated initially but later walked to where Ayo was and sat beside him.

'now' Alhaji began, 'I am aware that both of you hate me and might even kill me at the slightest opportunity'. He smiled.

'but haven't I been fair and nice to you as my guest'? Both men still kept quiet. Nosa who had not seen him before looked at Ayo and pointed to Alhaji.

'who is he……'? he asked

'am sorry, my name is Alhaji Abudu Mail; I guess you might have heard of me in the media.'

Nosa looked at him again and remembered everything about him. He was one of the richest if not the richest man in Africa.

'yes', he said nodding his head. 'I have heard much about you but what the hell are we doing here'?

Alhaji smiled again and lean forward.

'oh you mean your friend has not told you'? Nosa shook his head.

'alright, you'll be told but the doctor thinks your head is still arching……'

'noo am fine' Nosa interrupted him. 'please tell me why am being held here against my wish'.

Alhaji relaxed and crossed his legs.

'alright, don't let's push it okay?. Being an aeronautic engineer, we believe you will be of tremendous help to us here by taking care of our jets. If you co-operate with us, you will be paid three thousand dollars a day just like your friend here'.

Nosa stared at him and relaxed back in the chair in mute amazement. Alhaji was offering him a large amount of cash but that didn't bother him.

Money was not his problem as he was satisfied with what he had. But why will he be hiring him for such a thing and at such a cost, Nosa smelt danger.

'but why would you be offering me a job after you have kidnapped me and at such a price? Why didn't you just come to my office and do the negotiations'?

Alhaji looked at Ayo who was silent. He brought out one of his gold cigarette and lit it. Nosa stared at him as he smoked;

'answer me' he squealed.

Alhaji blew a thin cloud of smoke towards the ceiling

'keeping squealing' he said 'don't think about my offer, you just keep squealing'

Nosa stiffened; there was that look in Alhaji's eyes that looked devilish. Alhaji grinned when he saw fear in Nosa' eyes. They all fall for him when he gives them that his stone cold look. Ayo got up and switch on the TV, he wasn't going to watch them anymore. Nosa stared at Ayo and back to Alhaji;

'can someone in the room tell me what is going on'. Nosa asked, surprised his voice was still steady.

'plenty,' Alhaji said getting up he two quick steps to the door and turned;

'make sure you fulfill your side of the bargain'

'and if I don't accept your offer'?

'am afraid we will have to persuade you one way or another. And if you are planning on escaping, don't bother cos' there's no way out trust me'. Alhaji stepped out and slammed the door before Nosa could say any other thing.

'that guy is bluffing man' Nosa said turning to Ayo.

'he's not my friend, he means what he said'

'in that case, I will spoil and jam their radio system'

'that won't be a nice idea guy'.

'hehh?, why is that?' Ayo came to seat on the chair and looked at Nosa.

'the engineer they brought in here before tried that and they used a red hot knife to cut of his dick off and watch him bleed to death'.

Nosa looked at Ayo with horror in his eyes

'that's murder keee'.

'you are right Nosa, but it's called murder when seeking justice but it's treating your fuck up in an enclave like this'. Nosa looked at the TV then looked away. It wasn't going to be easy as he thought.

'ok Ayo fill me in with what is going on'. Ayo turned off the TV and turned his attention to Nosa.

'I think there is a coup in the offering'.

'what makes you think so'? Nosa asked his voice was now becoming unsteady

'the place they take me to every morning is stacked full with all sorts of military equipment you can ever imagine-tanks, trucks, assault vehicles, missiles, what have you'. Ayo looked at his hands, he was sweating, he rubbed the hands together and placed them on his knees.

'you know, sometimes I hear them talk about it'.

'sorry, I didn't get that last part. What are they talking about'?

Ayo looked at Nosa through his eyebrow and shook his head.

'it's like you are not understanding me, am saying that this bastard are staging a coup, war or something to topple the Nigerian government. They want to seize power and foment trouble in the land'.

Nosa blinked. He brought out his hanky with unsteady hands and cleaned his face. He looked at the hanky surprise there was no sweat, he cleaned the face again.

'have you gone mad'? he asked Ayo, 'how can you be saying a thing like that'?

'look Nosa I understand how you feel but that's exactly the news around here. So we need to play along in the mean time until we get a window'.

Nosa reasoned for some time and said;

'okay let's look at this thing closely, if they are staging a coup, that would have to be through the military, why stockpile arms'?

'that's the part difficult to understand. But who knows if this thing goes deep into the present administration'?

'gosh!!!' Nosa exclaimed 'I never knew this was loaded like this. But we need to look for a way to still warn the government'.

Ayo nodded his head and began to whisper.

'I've planned something, I know it might cost my life if they find out; but am not even sure I will be breathing when they are through with us'.

Nosa looked at Ayo narrowly and whispered back

'what's on your mind'?

'Not much, but the important thing is that I've sent a letter to Bisi; telling her about what is in the offering and that she gets help'.

'but how can they locate us when there is no address'? Ayo shrugged his shoulders;

'search me, but I think since I mentioned Alhaji's name, the government should be able to trace us'.

'that's smart but how do you post it'?

'one of the boys will be going to the post office tomorrow and I have slipped it into the mails. With luck, it would get to Bisi'.

'that's a smart move, let's hope and pray she gets it then'.

As Alhaji left Ayo and Nosa, a slim tall man came hurrying down the corridor.

'we've got company Alhaji' he said.

'come into my office' Alhaji snapped. They both hurried through the corridor and entered the office. Alhaji sat behind his desk and motioned him to sit down.

'okay Bodde, what's biting you'?

'sir, some men are in the plaza hotel. we believe they are from the Togolese government'.

Alhaji stared at him as if he just entered the room

'what do they want'?

'don't know yet sir but they've been making enquires relating to us but I don't think they've gotten any info; ve' assigned Hassan to cover their operation and the manager has also been alerted'.

Alhaji looked beyond Bodde, searched his brains and got up. He wandered to the window and paused.

'how long have they been in the hotel'?

'they checked in this morning sir'.

Alhaji leaned his back on the glass panel.

'how could they have traced us so fast' he said as if talking to himself Bodde shrugged his shoulders.

'listen' Alhaji said turning his attention on Bodde. 'I need you to handle this carefully. Make sure they live the building within the next hour and make sure Hassan stay on them even when they've gone'.

'I'll do that' Bodde said; he stood up and walked to the automatic door.

'Bodde', Alhaji called. Bodde paused by the door and turned back

'make sure this is done neatly'. Bodde said he will do just that and left the office. Alhaji was now deep in thought; they must have made a mistake somehow and somewhere but how? He had told Lawani to ensure nothing is traced back to them and he was sure Lawani did just that. Where is the leak coming from, could it be Bamidele or did the cleaners mix something? This was too fast for the Togolese government; he had thought they can buy time before they strike. He was going to look Bamidele over again and ask Lawani to verify all his movements. The cell phone interrupted his thought.

'yes'

'everything is now under control' Bodde said

'good' he hang up and a deadly smile animated his face. He knew Bodde was good in emergencies like this. That's why he put him as the head of his security. He raised the black telephone on his desk and dialed a number

'has Lawani come yet'

'yes sir' a soft beautiful female voice said. 'Bamidele is also just entering the building'.

'alright send them in' and he dropped the receiver. He brought out a bottle of Scottish wine, poured himself a drink and took it in a gulp. Alhaji knew he was taking a big risk if the Togolese government cannot find him; they would have to report to the Nigerian government. But that doesn't seem to bother him since no one knows of his involvement; he would be the last person the President will suspect. He poured another drink and this time, took a sip from the glass and set it on the desk. A tap came on the door he looked at the screen on the wall and saw Lawani and Bamidele. He pressed the button and the door swung open. They entered and Alhaji waved them to sit down.

'how did it go'? he asked

Lawani shook his head;

'nothing much Alhaji, the smugglers are having a hell of a time with the customs. So they were only able to get me two thousand bazookas, eight thousand hand grenades and twenty trucks.'

Alhaji nodded and turned to Bamidele.

'what about you'?

'they said their government has word out for them so they are lying low as it were. However, I was still able to get ten trucks with five loaded with arms and ammunitions'.

'well…. I, .. have decided that we attack next week. So Lawani sort out every necessary thing as we are good to go'.

'I agree with you' Lawani started leaning forward. 'after hearing the recent news from Bodde, I don't think it would be wise to wait any longer'.

'good' Alhaji said, he sipped from his drink and asked Bamidele ;

'any objections from you'.

'no. but about my sister…..'

'leave that issue for now Dele' Alhaji cut him short. 'we are in no mood for that, 've told you severally, your sister is fine'.

Lawani smiled and asked Alhaji

'I guess we should visit the ware house and assess our strength'

'yes, Lawani , let's do that tomorrow'. He asked Bamidele to leave them and Dele got up and went out.

CHAPTER NINE

It was 11am on Sunday morning. Bisi was inside the kitchen preparing breakfast while Ufan was lying on the sofa, reading a magazine in the living room. Bisi came into the living room and asked

'when did Emeka said he was coming'? Bisi asked coming out of the kitchen. Ufan shrugged her shoulders.

'search me, I don't know, morning or evening I guess, we are prepared. Bisi came to rest on the sofa.

'look Ufan, let me handle him alone okay'?

Ufan studied her for some time....

'ok girl, but I would have love to see those eyes pop out when you break the news to him. Only be very careful, you heard it yourself he is a killer'.

Bisi smiled.

'relax girl, I'll handle him like a child'. As Ufan turned her attention back to the mag, a cell phone began to ring.

'that's your cell phone' Ufan said

Bisi looked round to see where she had put it. The sound was coming from her hand bag on the center table. She opened the bag, brought out the phone and checked for the name of the caller. The caller id was showing unknown. Bisi hesitated for a moment before answering the call.

'hello' she said

'hello, it's me Emeka'. Bisi stiffened and looked at Ufan.

'how in the world did you get my number'? she asked. Ufan sat up.

'please let's not go into that; there's a slight change in plans. Let's meet at the Calvary hotel, we'll talk there'.

'ahhhhhh! but why, what made you change your mind'?

'nothing, you girls be there by twelve sharp' and the line went dead.

'was that Emeka'? Ufan asked

'yes'.

'how did he get your line'?

'ask me ooo my sister'. Bisi said throwing her hands in the air in frustration.

'this man is really a killer'. Ufan murmured. 'what did he say' she asked.

'he wants us at the Calvary hotel by 12pm'.

'anyway, whatever his tactics', Ufan said 'I think we have already bagged him'.

Bisi looked at her wrist watch.

'wooooooaaaa' she exclaimed, it's 11.20 already. Both girls hurried up and twenty minutes later, a Mercedes Benz E 300 was racing through the Benin Technical school road heading for the Calvary hotel.

'step on that pedal Ufan, we've to get there before him'.

Seven minutes later, Ufan pulled up in front of the gate, the Calvary hotel resort center was more of a night life place met for certain social class. It was towards the end of Benin Technical school road and it was at the out sketch. The resort center was always packed full with guests and tourist and the locals made their money from petty sells of suya, bottled groundnuts, coconut candies and all sorts of fresh fruits. The security guard raised the pole up and Ufan drove in; she parked the E 300 near an Audi A4 and both girls hurried out. Bisi put on her dark sunglasses that match with her yellow polo. She was putting on a combat shot with boots and a muffler round her neck. Ufan was wearing a T-shirt and a short hot faded jean skirt with a cross bag around her neck. They made their way into the reception hall with eyes staring after them. As they stepped into the hall, heads began to turn; there were two guys smiling at them trying to catch the girls' attention but they ignored them. Bisi looked round; she sighted a steward standing by a pillar in the hall staring at them. She beckoned on him, the steward took quick steps to meet them and grinned bowing a little.

'yes madam' he said 'how may I be of service'?

Bisi took off her sun glasses and said;

'we'll like to use a room for about thirty minutes, is any one free'?

'excuse me' the steward said and disappeared into the crowd. Since they came in Ufan had watched the front door, the steward appeared two minutes later with a key.

'room fourteen second floor'

'good now watch this door, when you see a big guy with two straight marks on his check, direct him to the room. Can you do that'?

'sssuure madam' he stammered but lingered. Bisi smiled and slipped three one thousand naira bills into his hands. The steward disappeared almost immediately. They made their way to the second floor and entered room fourteen. There were two big green sofas, a glass center table and a large bed. Ufan locked the door and sat on the bed while Bisi sat on one of the sofas. She dropped her bag on the table, brought out the cash inside and counted it; they were in a thousand naira bills.

'it will be a shock when Emeka sees these bills but can't touch them'. She chuckled and crossed her legs.

'it's almost twelve now and he's still not here' Ufan said ignoring Bisi. Just then a tap came on the door, Bisi motioned Ufan to open the door and place the cash back into the bag. Ufan got up and opened the door.

'you're right on time Mr. Emeka'. Ufan said

Emeka nodded and entered the room. Ufan followed him into the room and motioned him to sit on the sofa facing Bisi while she sat back on the bed.

'did you bring the pictures and the negatives'?

'of course, and you, is the money ready?' Emeka asked bringing out a brown envelop. He dropped it on the table where he could easily reach it and looked round the room.

'yes' Bisi said 'but let me remind you that this is cheap blackmail and you know it'.

Emeka looked at the two girls and shook his head.

'look, you girls murdered a man in cold blood and I happened to be in the vicinity and took a shot. I even helped you finished the job; so what have I done wrong here ehhh'?

'is that so'? Ufan asked

Emeka looked at them suspiciously and leaned back on the sofa.

'I don't know what you two are up to but let's make this exchange quick and go our separate ways is that not fair enough'?

'it isn't, not when you have the police on your trail'.

Emeka sat up abruptly.

'what are you driving at girl'?

'nothing, just feel that a wanted man like you shouldn't be the one calling the shots'

For a moment, Emeka felt hit by a moving car but he quickly recovered himself and laughed.

'look sisters, I have you two in my palm and you don't have any choice than to give me the money'.

Bisi shrugged her shoulders and motioned to Ufan who brought out the money from the cross bag and placed the dollar bills on the table. Emeka swallowed hard when he saw the bills; they were clean, fresh and neatly stacked.

'there you go', Bisi said 'forty million naira converted into dollars for ease of carriage. It's all yours if you've got the guts'.

Emeka looked at Ufan then at Bisi, he reached for the money and stop dead.

'I warned you 'bout leaving the police out of this didn't I; well since you won't play, watch out for the morning papers then'.

'just hand us the pictures and memory card' Ufan said.

'I believe you girls have been enjoying this but maybe you two don't know the shit you are in'

Bisi removed the muffler from her neck and relaxed on the sofa.

'listen Emeka', she started, 'you've got no other choice than to hand over the envelop'.

'well girls,' Emeka said getting up and picking up the envelop from the table.

'I think we'll better call it even since you want it your way'.

'hmmmmm, we can see you don't seems scared of the police'. Ufan said her voice as hard as steel.

'the police don't scare me, they are boys scout'.

'in that case will better call Dr. Okor that you don't seem to be scared of anyone'. Bisi said, a bite in her voice.

'what was that'? Emeka said surprised to see his voice and hands unsteady.

'don't mind Bisi'; Ufan said she wanted to tell you about Dr. Okor's daughter you kidnapped.

Although Emeka has been trained to absolve shock, he wasn't trained for this type. He reared backward, his morale faded away immediately, the room reeled before his eyes and the brown envelop dropped from his hands. The girls were enjoying themselves and it was with difficulty that they did not laugh. Here was one of the highest paid assassins under their control.

'don't panic Mr. Emeka' Ufan said trying to amuse herself; I'll advice you not to do blackmail when you have dirty things to hide. Emeka quickly recovered himself and without warning, a .45 caliber with a three inch silencer jumped into his hands.

'maybe I've not been too clear to you two but right now, you girls have gone too far; now hand the money over to me and none of you would get hurt'.

I will have to kill them anyway he thought, they know too much now. He wondered how they got such info 'bout him so fast. Ufan looked away while Bisi mumbled a curse.

'look Emeka' Bisi said standing up; 'you have no other choice now, let us help you. Killing us will still put you on the run; we can link you up with the police to take you in'.

'give me the money' he snarled 'or I'll have to take it and kill you two'.

Then it all happened in a second, Bisi docked to the left and threw a neat karat kick at him but Emeka saw the kick on time. He dock to the right as the .45 caliber coughed twice; the slugs buried themselves inside the sofa. Bisi cursed softly and threw a punch with all her weight behind it; the punch hit his lower jaw and sent him flying inside the room carrying the table with him. He crashed on the floor and the caliber fell from his hand. Ufan quickly jumped up and picked up the gun but Emeka was not done yet. He got up and launch at Bisi, raised her up and crashed her on the sofa; Bisi let out a groan and tried to standup.

'cut it off'! Ufan screamed aiming at Emeka. He turned to look at her and brought his attention back to Bisi. As he tried to heave Bisi from the sofa, Bisi delivered a head-butt on his nose and broke it, blood gushed out; Emeka tried to hold on to the nose but Bisi stood up and rushed him, she held him by his head and slammed it on the glass table scattering it.

'now that's enough' Ufan shouted 'no one is dying today'.

Emeka remained where he is, feeling defeated, he had some of the glass pieces on his face; he cursed himself for not being able to handle the girls. He had underestimated them too much. Bisi straighten her clothes and sat down on the other sofa, she opened her bag and threw Emeka a small towel.

'here, use this to stop the bleeding'. Ufan was still pointing the caliber at Emeka; she was not going to take any chance. She sat down quietly on the bed and looked at Bisi.

'are you okay' she asked

'yes am fine dear, thank you'.

Ufan turned to Emeka and said;

'look at the mess you have caused here now ehh'?

'alright, Emeka,' Bisi said, 'sit down and let's talk maturely'.

Emeka stumbled to sit down on the sofa. He was burning with fury inside him. He had hoped on these two girls as his ticket to leave the country and without thinking, he rushed towards Ufan on the bed but Ufan was expecting that move. She held up her legs for him to run into it and kicked him in his groins. Emeka let out a painful groan and fell back on the sofa.

'stop fussing around' Bisi snapped.

Emeka remained motionless for a minute or so then got up slowly and picked up the brown envelop from the floor. He dropped it on the floor in front of Bisi and sat down. Bisi picked it up and emptied the content on the sofa. They all stared at the pictures.

'are you sure this is all'? Bisi asked turning a cold eye on him.

'that's all there is'

'let's see your phone then' Ufan said. Emeka put his left hand into his pocket and Ufan raised the caliber. Slowly, he brought out the Samsung galaxy and gently tossed it to Bisi. She caught it and began to browse through.

'the pictures are not here' she said

'that's because 've Deleted all of them' Emeka said.

Both girls smiled. Here was one of the best assassins under their control. This would be a story to tell Bisi thought.

'now you are going to make a call' Bisi said softly

'to who' Emeka voice was unsteady

'to the Edo state police headquarters, they would be a better alternative to your boss'

How is that so'? Emeka asked rubbing his jaw.

'trust me', Bisi said. 'just ask for Mr. Latif; he's the Commissioner of police in the state, he will take you in'.

Ufan studied Emeka and pointed to the pictures;

'but you must leave out this' she said. 'after all we also have been helpful right'?

Emeka nodded his head and reached out for his cell phone, Bisi handed it over. He dialed a number and waited. He had thought of this as an alternative before now but was not sure if the Nigeria police would help. He knew the girls were right about calling the police as he had no future with Dr. Okor.

'this is Edo state police headquarters'; a female voice started, 'how can we be of service to you'?.

'please put me through to Chief Latif'

'and who is on the line please'?

'tell him it's Philip Emeka'.

There was a slight pause at the other end. Emeka could hear the heavy breathing of the female officer.

'are you sure you are who you claim to be'?

'yes, please put me through to him'.

'hold on a sec' the voice said. After a little delay, a rich voice came on the line.

'yes', the chief said politely.

'listen chief it's me Philip Emeka, I want to turn myself in though with a bargain of protection'. There was a little pause at the other end of the line then;

'alright, that can be arranged, just hang in there and tell us where you are so we'll come pick you up'. Emeka told the chief where he was and the chief said he will send a team to pick him up in the next five minutes. Emeka cut the line and looked at the girls;

'they will be here in five minutes'.

'that's fine with us, and you won't be needing this'? Ufan said waving the .45 caliber.

'nnoooo' he said shaking his head. He leaned forward, put his head down and held it in his hands.

'you people better go before they get here' he said.

Bisi collected the envelope with the pictures and they hurried out of the room.

'let's leave here before the place starts crawling with cops.' Ufan said as they raced down the staircase. They came out of the building and got into the car, as they drove out and joined the traffic, Bisi turned to catch a glimpse of six police cars entering the hotel.

'whoa, whoa, whoa' she said, 'the police is sure fast on this one; they really need this guy badly'.

Ufan shot the car forward and Bisi opened the envelope again, she brought the pictures and stared at them again.

'what an escape! She exclaimed; 'the cards are still falling our way'.

Ufan laughed out so loud the Benz E300 swerved slightly to the right.

'be careful' Bisi screamed holding on to the dashboard. These pictures would have spoilt so many things Bisi thought, talk about trust; Mr. Latif would have brought them in for serious scrutiny and questions and they would have been forced to give up all the info they have to the police. They were now approaching the University of Benin; Ufan slowed the car down, did a U-turn and pulled up in front of a shop opposite the main gate of the school.

'are you buy something'? Bisi asked

'yep, it won't take long'. Ufan got out and disappeared into one of the shops. Few minutes later, she appeared with some shopping bags and put them at the back seat. She got into the driver seat and thumbed the starter. She engaged the gear and slowly entered the Benin-Lagos express road again; as she got to the estate road, she turned right.

'so what's next'? Ufan asked when she pulled up in front of the gate.

'don't''ve a single clue girl' Bisi said getting out of the car, she opened the gates and Ufan drove into the car porch. Bisi quickly locked the gates and joined. They carried the shopping bags and went inside the house. Bisi came outside and checked the letter box; she beamed when she saw a letter but frown when she saw the letter addressed to her office with her official name Clara Ademolokun. She hurriedly tore the envelope, opened it and screamed.

'my goodness, talk of the devil, Ufan!!!!!!!!!!!!'

Ufan raced out of the house and they almost collided as Bisi was running inside.

'what in heavens are you screaming for'?

'it's Ayo, it's Ayo!!!!!' Bisi shouted with excitement weaving the letter in the air. They rushed inside sat on the sofa and with burning excitement they read the letter:

'Hello my love, Bisi.

It's me Ayo, am in trouble. If you get this letter, then there is hope that am still alive. I know you would have been looking for me, well I was kidnapped from my house the day I was to sign some documents for Mr. Ola. I was hit on the head from my back and by the time I woke, I found myself in an underground warehouse; though I don't know my location, I can only guess that am in the northern part. Bisi, I love you and the only way you can show your love is by looking for help. There is something terrible that is building up down here and I suspect a possible coup or civil war. Where I am been held is a huge stockpile of assorted military equipment and gadget ranging from armored tanks, assault vehicles, bazookas, MPGs, RPGs, trucks, AK47s etc. they even have some fighter jets and these equipment keep increasing by the day. I have been compelled to maintain their equipment after I received the beating of my life when I refused for the first few days.

'Bisi these dangerous people go by the name Amamadas and have been recruiting tactical teams and foot soldiers that have vowed to create mayhem in the country. They have begun to source for an aeronautic engineer as it appears that they are concluding plans to launch an attack.

You might not believe it but Alhaji Abudu is the architect of this group. There is also one Lawani and a very proud Bamidele and they have been getting help from outside the country. You will notice that I used Lawani's name on the address of the letter to deceive the guard carrying the mails. Remember, you need to get help and very fast and this should be treated top secret at the Federal level.

Remember, the fate of this country is now in your hands.

Ayo'.

After reading, Bisi and Ufan stared at themselves for a while and Bisi broke the silence as she heave a sigh of relief.

'at last!' She exclaimed. 'I have heard from him'. She looked at her hands and saw they were shaking. She tried to clasp them together but that didn't help.

've never trusted that Abudu of a person. There has always been something about him'.

'see what Ayo had to suffer. But why him?' she screamed throwing her hands into the air in desperation. She broke out in tears and held on to Ufan.

Ufan tried to hold her but she too was in tears.

'I guess we better start moving and go for help' Ufan said quietly. 'these tears won't help girl, let's move'.

Bisi cleaned her eyes and straighten up.

'you're right' she said 'but first let's destroy the pictures from Emeka before we head to Chief Latif'. Bisi took the pictures to the kitchen and set fire on them on the tiles. She washed her hands and came back to the living room to meet Ufan. Bisi picked up the phone receiver and began to dial a number.

'are you thinking what am thinking Ufan?'

Ufan looked up abruptly and got up

'no they can't pick Nosa, no they just can't' she said.

They waited with eagerness but the line was ringing continuously at the other end without any answer. Ufan grabbed the phone receiver from Bisi, cut the line and dialed Nosa's office.

'heelo' she said when the line came through. 'Please is Nosa around'?

'no' the other voice said. 'He's gone on vacation'.

Ufan slammed the receiver on the cradle.

'they've got him'. she said.

'you can't be so sure yet' Bisi said. She picked up the receiver again and dialed the Nigerian Union of scientist secretariat and waited reluctantly.

'hello' a soft voice said 'this is the Nigerian Union of scientist secretariat what can we do for you'?.

'hello, this is Bisi, please, is Nosa there?'

'no he has gone on vacation but he was here a week ago to sign some documents'. Ufan gnawed her fingers impatiently.

'please let me speak to Mr. Ola' she said to Bisi. Bisi told the secretary that she wanted to speak to Mr. Ola.

'hold on' the voice said and after a slight delay Mr. Ola voice came up.

'hello Bisi'

'it's me, Ufan sir'. Collecting the telephone receiver from Bisi

'ahhhhh Ufan!!!!' Ola said in a surprised voice. 'I thought you and Nosa were on vacation together'.

Ufan stiffened and quickly checked herself. If Ola got a wind of the news, that would be it.

'you're right' she said 'but I changed my mind. Your secretary said Nosa was in your office a week ago'?

'that right'

'did you see him ever since then?'

'why, ve' not seen him since then. ehheh is there any problem?'

'nnnoo sir, not at all I just wanted to be certain he signed the papers before he left'. Bisi signaled Ufan she wanted to talk to Ola and Ufan handed the phone back to her.

'hello sir'.

'oh! Bisi how are you doing'?

'am fine sir. Ayo called yesterday and asked me to tell you he will sign the papers when he comes back'

'that's alright. Did you receive the letter I dropped in your mail box?'

'ohh yes I did sir, thank you so much. See you later sir'. Bisi dropped the receiver before Ola could say other word.

'They've got him' Ufan said surprise her voice was steady.

CHAPTER TEN

In the Togolese capital, Mr. Clifo, Chume and Dr. Chandler were discussing how far the agents have gone when the telephone rang. Dr Chandler who was close to the phone picked it up.

'hello' he said into the receiver

'what news do you have for me'. A commanding and threaten voice demanded. Recognizing the voice of the President, Dr. Chandler sat up.

'we're trying to locate them sir but our boys have not been successful sir'.

'meaning what'? the president shouted.

'sir, since we are yet to get their location, we can't report anything to the Nigerian government because the information that they are Nigerians might be wrong'.

Dr. Chandler could hear the heavy breathing of the Togolese President at the other end of the line.

'okay, send the boys back there and if they can't still find them, we'll have to report to the Nigerian government anyway; is that understood?'

Dr. Chandler told him he understood and waited for the President to cut the line before he replaced the receiver carefully.

'the President has turned the heat on' he said quietly. 'any ideas Mr. Chume'?

Chume shook his head and said he had nothing to say.

'listen to me' Clifo started learning forward

'we are facing a very difficult task here. Nigeria is a neighbour that we must protect her interest if we want peace, so the only way out of this jam is to report the matter to the Nigerian government'.

'no' Chandler said shaking his head. 'we don't even have evidence that this people are Nigerians or planning to cause violence in the country. We need hard rock evidence if our story is to sell and let me remind you that we are interested in the tanks and not the people'.

'Chandler is right' chume said nodding to clifo. 'whoever is in charge of the Nigerian government should be capable to take care of their problems we are more interested in the tanks'.

Clifo relaxed back in his chair and shrugged his shoulders.

'if that's what you guys think, then its good, am with you but remember that we'll be on the streets if this whole exercise turns sour'.

'yeh yeh, am quite aware of that' chandler said 'but let's see what the boys will come up with this time before we draw the curtain'.

Lawani Peters sat in his office in a relaxed mood; he smiled to himself as he inhaled the nicotine and puff the smoke to the roof. Alhaji was right he thought, they would have to strike now or risk losing the war they have invested so much in; that would be a collateral loss coupled with the billions Alhaji already owned, after all that was the purpose of the war plans in the first place. As Alhaji's right hand man, he knew of the bad investment his boss has made and how the banks have been threatening him. It won't be long before the issues becomes public and Alhaji Abudu falls like a pack of cards and his extensive financial empire collapse like a building with faulty pillars. Lawani believed nothing in the world can stop them now. They'll have to hide under the Geneva conventions and other rules of engagement to perpetuate the war. Alhaji had carefully planned out this strike and there was no way anyone in the country will know about his involvement. Plans have already been put in place to lure in some terrorist groups and some of the drug lords when the war begins; and when that happens, they will withdraw to their bunkers and just sell arms. Alhaji will be back in business again like during the civil war. Despite the fame and wealth Alhaji had made all over the world, the money was still not enough. What is wrong to make more money and be the richest man on earth? Is that position only met for the Americans, Arabs and Asians? He paused to mix a soda and whiskey for himself and resumed his thought. He thought about their arsenals, he was sure they were just waiting for the go light before they can unleash terror on the country. Even if the arms were not enough, the insurgents would make the war tougher for arms trade to strive. Lawani gulped the drink and mixed another one, he was not going to get involved in the war neither will Alhaji. All they need to do was make some damaging strikes in strategic areas across the country, sponsor some media groups to blame some terrorist groups and wait for the chaos to start. Then they would have to keep out of sight and monitor things from their base. He sipped from the alcohol and looked at the glass as if he was served by a waiter. Bamidele was another headache; he would have to take care of. He could see that Alhaji had begun having soft spot for him and he wouldn't want that. But what if their plans turn soar, he thought. He shook his head and said aloud to himself;

'we will win this war' he said aloud as if arguing with an opponent. He opened his desk drawer and brought out a file. He then switched on his lap top and begun to carefully compare the data in the file and the system. The intercom buzz and Lawani leaned forward to answer it.

'yes'?

'Bodde and Bamidele is here sir' the secretary said.

'just a minute'

He went through the data again. Satisfied every data was accurate; he switched off the laptop and kept back the file in the drawer.

'ok' he said into the intercom; 'send them in'

Two minutes later, Bodde and Bamidele entered the office. Bamidele offered his hand as he came to rest by the desk.

'hello guys', Lawani said standing up to take his hand.

'how are you doing sir'? Bodde asked

'good, good, please sit down'. They sat down and Lawani brought out two glasses from his drawer and set them on the desk.

'Help yourself'.

'thanks' Bamidele said and poured some whiskey for himself and Bodde. Bamidele was putting on a black suit, white tie dotted with black and a hat. He removed the hat, sipped from his drink and lit a cigar. Lawani looked at him and smiled; sooner or later, he would be very dead he thought. He smiled again at his dressing; Bamidele always liked to dress in a corporate fashion. Lawani stood up, walked to the cabinet and brought out a bottle of Irish whiskey. He set it on the desk and pushed it to them.

'help yourselves' he said, 'we've got to start celebrating'. Bodde reached for the whiskey and mixed it with his former drink. He too was wearing a black suit but his tie was a red.

'there's something that still puzzle me' Bamidele started, if we want to strike, were do we start from'?

Lawani grinned and sipped his drink.

'that's Alhaji's prerogative boy'.

'is Alhaji around'? Bodde asked

'yes, in his office, anything'?

'Plenty, first of all, the Togolese agents are back into the state and instead of the five that came the last time, they are now eight.'

Bamidele sat up and Lawani's grin went away like an opened door. He raised his hand as a gesture to Bodde to hold on.

'Alhaji must hear this' he said. He raised the telephone receiver up and leaned back.

'yes' Alhaji's deep voice said

'Bodde and Bamidele are with me, please I need you here. It's urgent'.

'what' biting you, tell me now'

'it's the Togolese, they are back'. Lawani said knowing Alhaji hate suspense.

The line went dead and Lawani dropped the receiver.

'he's coming'. Bodde nodded his head and emptied the alcohol into his mouth. The automatic door behind Lawani swung open and Alhaji came inside the office. He was putting on a navy blue safari and a black Italian sandal. He took a chair, sat close to Lawani and crossed his legs.

'Bodde just told me that the Togolese are back in the state'.

Alhaji turned his attention to Bodde.

'when did you get this info'?

'this morning'

Alhaji folded his hands together and asked

'how many are they'?

'eight' Bamidele said. Alhaji looked at him as if he had not been in the room.

'where are they now' he asked turning his attention back to Bodde. Bodde shrugged his shoulders

'you mean you people don't know where they are'? Alhaji barked. Bodde shook his head

'then how come you know they are in the state already?' Alhaji was fighting to control his rage.

'the hotel manager told me. He said he recognized three of the agents. He stated that the agents insisted on lodging in the hotel but he told them there were no more rooms.'

'what about Paul that was assigned to them' Lawani interrupted.

've since called him off when the agents were suspicious of him'. Alhaji nodded his head and got up and came round to lean on the edge of the desk and crossed his legs

'listen' he said, we've already decided about this war. Come rain or shine, we are already in. This is the moment to strike before this sick Togolese gives us problems'.

Lawani cleared his throat.

'you are right Alhaji', he said 'lets' fix a date and forget about the Togolese.' Bamidele crushed his cigar in the ash tray. He knew this moment will come one day; though he knew that Alhaji and Lawani allowed him into their caucus, he knows it was only because his sister is being held. And he was sure she would be in the warehouse building they occupy at Kaduna. That is the only place they can keep her he thought. He was also aware that he will need to watch out for Lawani who would take killing him as a pleasure.

'am in this with you people' he said. 'just tell me the day and that's all I need. Lawani grinned.

'for a moment, I thought you were going to say something different. What about you Bodde'?

'no objections' Bodde said, 'but I still have some bad news to break'.

Alhaji looked at Bodde suspiciously while Lawani stiffened.

'what is it about you and bad news'? Alhaji snapped.

It's about Obakpolor, the Edo state police has somehow linked him with Owa Omoruyi and his team.' Alhaji almost jumped off the desk, he looked at his hands and was surprised they were still steady. Slowly, he left the desk went round and sat down. Lawani mixed another soda with the Irish whiskey he brought out and took it in a gulp.

'I think am going to get myself drunk' he said. Alhaji looked at him and turned his attention back to Bodde.

'what's wrong with you Bodde, please snapped up the story'.

'the police said they are still investigating but they believe that Obakpolor was also on a mission in the state when he died; they've dropped the suicide story'.

'Bisi!!!' Lawani exclaimed 'that girl is sure up to something. I believe she was the one that made it look like suicide in the first place; she is sure at the middle of all this'.

'what happened after that' Alhaji asked as if Lawani had not spoken

'they are still investigating and have traced Obakpolor's house to Kaduna and as we speak; the Kaduna police have joined them to search the house'.

'I thought we took care of that'? Alhaji asked

'sure we did' Bodde said. Alhaji nodded his head and turned to Bamidele.

When did this story come in'?

'about 30 minutes ago' Bamidele said adjusting his tie and trying to meet Alhaji's searching eyes.

'well, there is no going back now' Alhaji said, 'we will need to strike and create a hellish atmosphere.'

He looked round the room and they all nodded their heads.

'okay then, let's go to the ware house'.

CHAPTER ELEVEN

The powerful search light on the wall woke Ayo Lewis. He rolled out of bed and went into the bathroom; that was his routine. He still felt dizzy from the short sleep he had in the night as he was with Nosa almost through the night. It took him twenty minutes to shave and take his bath. As he came out of the bathroom, Bobbo came in with his food. He was a big hairy man with a small head but he had large shoulders.

'good morning Ayo'

'morning, how are you today'?

'fine, am sorry I had to wake you earlier than usual. We are expecting Alhaji and his team this morning and I will want them to meet everything in order'.

Ayo nodded his head. He raised the stainless steel cover up and peeped at the food. There was five slices of bread, a small mayonnaise bottle and a stick of cucumber; he moved to the cabinet, mixed a scotch and vodka and put it on the table close to the food. Bobbo grinned, turned and walked to the door.

'I will come and pick you in fifteen minutes please'.

He paused by the door and looked back. Ayo said he would be ready and Bobbo left the room. As he ate, Ayo began to wonder what must be going on that Alhaji and his team is coming to see. For three days now the work has been intense in the warehouse and the traffic has also been heightened. He was sure this people are rounding up their plans to attack. He was also sure that Bisi would have gotten the letter since it did not come back. Bisi was the only hope he and Nosa had now to stop Alhaji and his cohorts. The tap on the door interrupted his thought. Nosa opened the door and came inside.

'have you heard the news'? he asked closing the door.

Ayo nodded his head and swallowed the remains of the cucumber.

'but I thought Alhaji had his office in this building'.

'no' Ayo said 'Bobbo recently told me he is staying in Yola while we are in Kaduna.' Nosa was taken aback for a moment. He looked at Ayo in mute amazement.

'you mean we were carried all the way from Edo state to Kaduna'.

'hhhmmmm' Ayo said nodding again.

'I think we'll better start planning a way of escape boy; I have a feeling our days here are numbered'.

Nosa nodded in agreement

'you are right but first we need to look for a way of getting hold of some weapons at least.'

Ayo stood up and motioned him to the bedroom. He raised the mattress up and gestured at Nosa. Nosa looked at the broad sheet of paper and back to Ayo

'what's that'? he asked in a whisper

'the building plan. Please don't ask me how I got it'

'okay let's attend to this idiots first and when we get back, we'll sit down and plan'.

'no qualms' Ayo said. 'but see if you can lay hands on some weapons you think we will need before the close of the day'. Just then they heard the door of the first room open; and Bobbo was calling.

'okay fellows, it's time to work'. They came out of the room and followed bobbo through a corridor on the left.

'Alhaji would be happy with you two when he comes'.

Why is that so'? Nosa asked.

Bobbo looked back at Nosa;

'you two have done a great job, why will he not be happy'?

Ayo looked at Nosa. Bobbo was now talking as if they have finished their services with them. They remained silent as they walked down the corridor. At the end of the corridor, they stopped and bobbo brought out his card and inserted it into the device by the door; the door came apart and they stepped into a large hall. It was stockpiled with assorted military equipment and gadgets. Bobbo grinned and pressed a hidden button and the doors came together again.

'well, you guys start working, there will be no long hours today. Just cross check everything you've done so far before Alhaji comes in.'

Bobbo pressed the electric bell and workers began to troop in from the other end of the hall. He let out a chuckle, he always liked to address people and act the boss.

'now listen up' he said raising his voice a little, 'you all know Alhaji is coming in this morning for inspection, is everything ready'?

'yes sir' the workers chorused. Bobbo turned to Ayo;

'do you have anything to say to them'?

'yesterday' Ayo started, I asked you to oil the guns. Have you done that'?

'yes we did.' a tall slim elegant girl said

'very well then, I don't think there will be much work today'.

'what about you' bobbo asked turning to Nosa

I don't think I really have much, but we'll like to see the pilots'.

'that would be arranged' bobbo said inspecting some of the MPGs lined up on a rack. 'now please let's start work'

Ayo and Nosa went to work. Ayo went through all the arms on the racks; he kept frowning at the sight of the arms. He began to wish they were never invented. He paused to admire the Chinese made T-64 tank and examined it closely. It was one of the sophisticated weapons in the warehouse and they numbered about eighty. He passed the tanks and came to the roll of AK47; they will certainly be useful he thought. He checked one of them and was surprised it was loaded. Opposite the roll of AK4 where about fifteen assault vehicles, Ayo climbed one and checked the wicked looking gun mounted on top of it, he raised his eye lids as it too was loaded; they had not been loaded as at yesterday when they were in the warehouse. On his part, Nosa inspected the fighter jets with so much pains and annoyance burning inside him. He frowned at the thought of even helping an organization that was bent on causing havoc on the country; but there was nothing he can do now as he was trapped. He hoped that Ayo's letter would reach the authorities and help would be dispatched. He knew that very soon their services will no longer be needed and that was why they would need to make a quick move on escape.

After some 50 minutes, Ayo and Nosa where relaxing and taking a bottle of coke when bobbo came in with one of the pilots;

'you asked for the pilots right, well here you are' he said. Nosa forced a smile and beckon to the pilot.

'why didn't you bring all?' he asked

Bobbo shrugged his shoulders and laughed.

'pardon me buddy, that's one of my bad habits'.

''what's your name'? Nosa asked the pilot

'don't bother for his name' a deep croak voice said behind them. Ayo and Nosa turned. Standing about ten feet away from them was Alhaji, Lawani and two others. Alhaji stretched out his right hand as they walked towards Ayo and Nosa.

'good morning my friends' he said as he shook them. 'I hope we didn't take you guys by surprise'?

'ohh nooo' Ayo said 'we were informed of your coming'

'good' Alhaji smiled and rubbed his hands together. He turned to Nosa.

'let me introduced you to my friends'. He brought out a white handkerchief and wiped his face.

'this' he began pointing to Lawani , 'is Lawani Peters and he is my right hand man'

Nosa shook hands with him.

'and these other two, are Bodde and Bamidele '. Nosa nodded to them, studied the one carrying a laptop bag he thought his face looked familiar and looked away.

'let's discuss in the office' Lawani said heading to the door marked private. They walked into the room quietly. Alhaji sat on the chair behind the desk and Bamidele placed the laptop bag on the desk. Ayo and Nosa waited for the others to seat before taking their own seats. Alhaji brought out the laptop from the bag and set it on the desk.

'pardon us gents, we need an update'; he said

Ayo leaned back on the chair and took his time. This was the time for them to act according to their plans.

'well'? Alhaji said quietly. Ayo forced a smile and looked at him directly.

'the equipment are good to go. I can assure you that everything inside the warehouse is in perfect order. But what happened to the guided and short range missiles'?

'why are you asking such a questions'? Lawani queried

'take it easy' Alhaji said to Lawani and turning to Ayo he said;

'I would advise that you don't bother about that. But if you must know, they have been placed in strategic locations across the country'.

Both Ayo and Nosa could not absorb the shock; they almost jumped out of their skins. Alhaji smiled he was enjoying himself no doubt. He waited for them to recover from the shock then he turned his attention to bobbo.

'how far have you gone with the boys'?

'they are ready sir'. Bobbo said. Alhaji nodded his head and turned to Bamidele .

'do you have anything to say'? Bamidele said he had nothing to say.

'what about you'? he asked Bodde. Bodde shook his head

'okay guys, let's check the warehouse'. They stood up and went into the warehouse; Ayo and Nosa took their time to take them through the entire armory. When they were through, Alhaji patted the duel on their backs.

'you too have done very well' he said; 'my friends and I are deeply grateful to you'.

Nosa caused under his breath, he thought of killing Alhaji if given the slightest chance to do so. Lawani caught the look and smiled.

'and what is on your mind'? Lawani asked.

'I was just thinking how I would kill you guys if I have the opportunity'. Lawani and the rest roared in laughter 'get that of your chest' Lawani said trying to catch his breath.

'after all the way we have treated you two, why would you think of killing us'? Alhaji asked

'you people had never liked us' Ayo began looking directly at Alhaji; we know you are just pretending until you are done with us......'

'that's not true' Bodde cut in; 'if you think we've not been good to you do you think Alhaji would have offered to be paying you fifteen thousand a day'?

'is the money by hand or through the bank'? Ayo queried.

'it's alright', Alhaji said. 'We'll pay you your money as soon as your work is over.'

There was a temporal silence. Ayo looked at Bamidele who was just smiling; he hissed and spat on the floor. Bamidele was the worst of them all he thought. Ayo knew what he was made of; he was sort of the guy that fixes things. He would sure be the first he would fall if ever he had the opportunity.

'you guys can now leave us'. Alhaji said breaking the silence; Nosa and Ayo looked at themselves and made for the door.

'we'll call you guys if the need arises' Lawani said as the automatic doors closed behind the duel. Alhaji turned his attention to the rest in the hall.

'I hope you all are in high spirits now'.

'am ready' Bodde said balancing an AK47 in his hands. He raised the gun to the roof and pulled the trigger. The hall became alive with the burst of gun fire; the slugs hit the bullet proof ceiling. Lawani let out a burst of laughter and his Mauser with a 3'inch silencer jumped into his hands. He aimed at an energy bulb on the ceiling, the gun coughed twice and they all entered another round of laughter as the bulb was shattered.

'now listen' Alhaji said. 'It's time to fix a date for the strike; we don't want the Togolese drawing the rug under our feet'.

'my men are ready' Bodde started; 'we just need the date and time'

'that goes for me' bobbo said learning on one of the pillars. Alhaji nodded and turned to Lawani .

'what day do you suggest'?

'next week Tuesday'

'is that okay by you all'? they nodded their heads. Alhaji nodded again and turned to bobbo.

'you are in charge of all the missiles. I will tell you their locations later'.

'it will be taken care of'. bobbo assured.

'good' and you Alhaji said pointing to Lawani ; 'you are to monitor the armory and also be in charge of the troops'. Lawani nodded his head.

Bamidele will control the ship and sub while Bodde will take charge of the jets; any questions'?.

'where are the ship and subs'?

Bamidele asked.

Alhaji turned to Lawani . He cleared his throat twice.

've' infiltrated and mixed the ship in the dock yard with that of the government'. Bamidele nodded his head and grinned but deep down inside him, he wasn't satisfied. Lawani himself knew that the ship would not be able to do the damage they wanted. They all knew they were weak in the sea and that is why Bamidele is to handle that area. They would only hope for the insurgency and militants to fuel the crisis when they attack.

Bisi and Ufan were in the national Museum in a quiet corner and had been talking in hush tones about Ayo and Nosa for about thirty minutes now. The water fountain was behind them and the crowded guests as well as the noise of the vehicles going round the king's square were all hushed as they were deep in thoughts. Ufan had recovered from the shock that Nosa was also missing. She took her mind back to what they have done before now. They had burnt the brown envelop which Philip had given them and went straight to Nosa's house and found the place empty. With her spare key, they had made their way into the house and found the place as silent as a grave yard. Apart from the noise of the birds from the trees in the compound, the entire house was silent. They also noticed that the house has been thoroughly searched and some of his personal effects taken away. They had left the place and had driven straight to the Museum and sat under the large Christmas tree trying hard to believe what is happening.

'what exactly should we do right now'? Ufan asked

Bisi shrugged her shoulders, crossed her legs and said;

'time for the police I guess'

'those bastards' Ufan said between her locked teeth. 'we'll teach them a lesson'

'of course, of course but that will be when we find them.' Ufan looked at Bisi and smiled a deadly smile.

'oohh we'll find them alright, even if we have to turn this country upside down, we'll sure find them and smoke them outs'. Bisi glanced at Ufan and looked away. She knew Ufan had nerves like steel and Bisi liked her for that. She put her hand on Ufan's hand and patted it affectionately.

'don't you worry sister, we'll get them but first let's plan out what to tell the police so we'll be relevant when it gets the Federal attention'.

Ufan nodded in agreement.

'first of all' Ufan started, we must leave out Obakpolor's case and must have good reasons for keeping this info from the appropriate authorities ever since'.

'you are on course Ufan, but the police needs to know the whole story especially as it relates to Obakpolor…..'

'no way Bisi'; Ufan cut in, 'Obakpolor story must be Deleted. Have you gone crazy or what? What if the police treat it as a murder case?'

Bisi looked at Ufan and grinned.

'listen to me Ufan, that is not murder and you know it. Anyway I do not think the chief would have problems with that. I think it's better for us to lay our cards on the table before they find out things themselves'.

'what makes you think they will ever find out about Obakpolor if we don't tell them? They already called it suicide, come on Bisi'.

'Emeka might crack you know'

'alright Bisi, you win. You do the talking and remember to talk us out of the reason why we were holding on to all the info at our disposal'.

'just leave that to me. The chief has given me his word and come to think of it the weight of Ayo's letter would dictate the pace, trust me.'

Ufan studied Bisi for a while and relaxed on the chair.

'okay prof., when do we see the chief'?

'we'll see him first thing tomorrow morning. I guess mornings are better for shockers like this'.

Ufan began to reflect on their past adventures right from when Bisi escaped her kidnappers to the way they handled Obakpolor and Emeka. She smiled to herself and closed her eyes.

'what's funny, what are you smiling for'? Bisi asked

'just thinking of our past adventures'

Bisi looked at her, for a moment, she was confused and then she realize what Ufan was talking about.

'our adventures had been good isn't it? Luck had been on our side from the start'.

Bisi got up and pulled Ufan up to her feet.

'come on girl, time to go home'.

They walked through the crowd quietly and made their way to the Toyota Rav 4. They got in and as they drove out of the museum, Bisi watched a Nissan Premiere wagon suspiciously for some time before she entered Adesogbe road. Satisfied that they were not being followed, she crossed the Ekewan road, took the car through the Ehaekpen road and headed for the New Lagos road.

CHAPTER TWELVE

Ayo Lewis got up and switch off the radio. Today was the D-day he said to himself. He crossed the room and went into the bathroom; removed the mirror from the wall and brought out two AK47 rifles from the hole he had dug there. He grinned as he examined them, they were fully loaded.

'Nosa and I would need you' he said patting the rifles. He brought out his handkerchief and cleaned them carefully. This so called Amamadas would sure be in for a surprise he said to himself. He carried the rifles to the bed and dropped them carefully as if they were made of egg shells. He bent low, raised the rug carpet and brought out two .45 colt automatic with a 3' inch silencer from under the rug. There was no going back now he thought; he was sure their stay was on borrowed time and he was determined to die on his feet than on his knees. He raised the telephone receiver by the side of the bed and dialed three digits.

'hello' Nosa said almost immediately.

'can I see you for a moment'?

'of course, I'll be with you in a jiffy'.

Ayo replaced the receiver and looked round the room. He then put the weapons under the bed and came to the living room. Apart from the R&B music coming from the next room, the living room was silent. He opened the front door, left it ajar and went back into the room. A moment later, Nosa came in, locked the door and went into the inner room with a kit bag. Ayo beamed and helped Nosa with the bag. They emptied the contents on the bed and stepped back.

'whaoooo what do you have here'? Ayo exclaimed in a hushed voice.

'these are the things I could get'

'this will do' Ayo said examining them. There were two .45 colt automatic, six magazines for the AK47, four knives, two black jackets and berets, two pairs of hand gloves and four grenades.

'did you lock the front door properly'?

'yes I did' Nosa replied massaging his jaw. 'where are the ones with you'?

Ayo brought them out from under the bed and Nosa smiled for the first time since entering the room. He brought out a map and the plan of the building and spread them on the bed.

'now here's the stuff. I've gone through more than I can remember'. Ayo studied the map and plan for some time and looked up.

'explain our movement to me'.

Nosa nodded and placed the plan on the map.

'let me explain this first. When we leave this room, we'll take the corridor on our right; instead of the left Bobbo use to take us through every morning'. He paused as Ayo went to get two canned stout drink, they opened the can and drank from it. Nosa set his can on the stool close to the bed and continued;

'the corridor on the right is a little bit long and there are three guards guiding the corridor. At the end of the corridor, we'll branch out to the right again. This path is short but there are about four guards there. At the end of the corridor is an elevator which will take us to the top floor'.

Nosa paused again, emptied the rest of the content inside his mouth and toss the can on the rug. He was feeling uneasy as Ayo was drinking while he had been the one talking.

'so what happens at the top floor'? Ayo asked causally.

'there are five guards at the top floor; two of which guide the elevator, one of the remaining three guide the main door leading outside and the other two are out there hiding somewhere. With luck, there might be a car or something outside that we can use to escape'.

Ayo gulped the rest of the drink, threw the can into the empty trash can. He picked up the plan and studied it more carefully; it was not going to be easy he told himself but there was no better choice now; it was a necessary risk they must take. After a minute or so, he dropped the plan and went into the living room. He came back with a flagon and two glasses after serving himself and Nosa, he sat on the bed and took a sip from his glass.

'how did you get this Intel'? he said staring directly at Nosa.

'hehhhh!!!!! Boy, relax don't worry 'bout that ok'?

'no I insist, I want to know exactly how you got it'?

'alright, remember you gave me the plan, then I got the map from my guard. I told him I wanted to study it and would return it; as for the Intel, he also told me about it'.

Ayo dropped the glass and looked at him suspiciously.

'haba! how come the guard just told you everything'?

Nosa grinned and licked his lower lip.

'I persuaded him to tell me'

'what about the arms'

'ohh I got those from the warehouse myself; you got yours from there didn't you?".

Ayo looked at him and smiled.

'so you killed the guard ehh'?

'he made me to'

'how did you do it'?

Nosa grimaced and spat on the rug.

'I broke his neck'

'hmmmm, that means our time here is up; soon they would start looking for him'

'okay let's snap this up' Nosa said,

He collected the map and plan, put it inside the kit bag and put it under the mattress. They quickly got dressed with the gloves, jacket and beret. They packed up the things from the bed and loaded the magazines and grenades into their jacket. They hung each of the AK47 at their backs, and stuck the .45 automatic on their belts with one each left in their hands and three minutes later, they were ready.

'before we go' Ayo said adjusting his hand gloves. 'how are the guards positioned and what is the nature of the corridor'?

'they move in twos and the corridor is winding so we stand a chance of seeing them before they see us'.

Ayo nodded his head. This will be a great surprise for the Amamadas. He checked the .45 automatic again, satisfied it was fully loaded, he pulled the safety catch; Nosa did the same.

'are you ready'? Ayo asked

'just like in the moves right'?

'yeah boy but this is real, no film tricks. Please keep yourself alive to tell this story okay'?

they hugged themselves passionately.

'remember Nosa, we are not dying today'.

'okay' Nosa said 'let's go'. They came out from the room entered the living room. The R&B was still playing, that was the blind Nosa planned for the guards on patrol to think he was fast asleep. Ayo opened the door quietly and poke out his head the corridor was empty and quiet; he came out cautiously and beckoned to Nosa who quickly joined him. They raced fast but silently through the corridor and stopped when they got to one of the bends. Nosa poked his head out just in time to see the guard who was almost at the bend; he docked back and with his left hand, brought out his knife that gleamed under the energy bulb in the corridor. Without looking at their direction, the guard strolled passed them. Nosa smiled and launch at him, he drove the blade deep into his neck just above the collar bone and twisted the blade twice while covering his mouth with his right hand. The guard left out a groan and Nosa guided him gently as he slumped down. Ayo quickly grabbed his legs and dragged him to a door. Nosa opened the door cautiously and Ayo pulled him inside. Nosa cleaned the blade on the corpse and closed the door quietly. They continued their movement.

'keep your eyes opened' Nosa said in a whisper; 'the other guards walk in twos'.

Ayo nodded his head but stopped as he heard voices. He looked at Nosa who gestured to him that the voices might be from the two guards. They hid themselves behind the next bend and waited patiently. Killing the guards was not murder but pure self-defense Ayo thought. The guards came round the bend and stood dead when they saw them. Even if their jobs were to resist intruders, this duel was the last they expected to see. Before the guards could regain their shock, Ayo .45 automatic coughed twice and one of them fell forward. Nosa launched forward and delivered a wicked judo kick on the other's neck; as he fell down he hit him again and broke his neck. They dragged them into the nearest room and closed the door.

'the guards here are finished'. Nosa said quietly. Ayo nodded and they made their way to the end of the corridor occasionally looking back. They branched to the right and walked softly as if the floor was laid with zinc. There were two guards about ten feet away their backs towards them; while one paused to lit a cigar, the other moved ahead. Ayo motioned Nosa to take care of the one with cigar while he takes care of the other one. Before the guard could finish lighting his cigar, he felt a sharp thing inside him and when he say his blood, he was too surprise to shout. He gave out a little groan of pain and dropped to the ground. The other guard swung round when he heard the groan but he was too late, Ayo delivered a flying karate kick on his neck and broke it instantly. There were no doors in the part of the corridor so they quickly crossed them and raced down the corridor to the last bend. They peeped and saw two guards about twenty feet away from them; one was sitting behind a desk lost in thought and the other was learning on the wall reading a magazine. There was no way they could get to the guards without them seeing them. Ayo looked at Nosa with bewilderment. Nosa whispered to Ayo softly;

'this has been the part I couldn't solve when I got the Intel'

'don't sweat' Ayo whispered back; 'we 'll aim them from here, you take the one behind the desk and I'll take the other one'.

'fair enough' Nosa whispered he aimed at the head and squeeze the trigger. The .45 colt hissed and the guard let out a shout, heaved forward and his body fell on the desk; his blood quickly spread on the papers on the desk.

The other guard quickly dropped his magazine and reached out for his machine gun tangling on his neck but he never had the opportunity to fire it. Ayo shot him between the eyes as he ran towards him. The gunman spread out in full length on the floor. They quickly raced towards the elevator and got in. as the doors closed, they looked at the corpses and the blood all over the place. The elevator rode to the top floor and stopped.

'this part is going to be very tricky' Nosa said.

As the doors swung open, two guards standing in front of the door saw them their mouth wide open; without hesitation, Ayo and Nosa shot them and they died in their surprise. They crossed the corpses and raced towards the front glass door but the guard there saw them first. He raised his machine gun and opened fire as he threw himself on the floor screaming. Nosa cursed under his breath and they hid behind two opposite pillars. The guard kept firing knowing he was in the open but sooner than he thought his magazine was empty. He quickly brought a Mauser, stood up and made for the glass door.

'we need to move before the entire building come all out on us'.

Ayo nodded he pulled out his AK47 rifle, sprang out from behind the pillar and began firing sporadically. The slugs perforated the guard and scattered the glass door; the guard fell with a heave screaming on top of his voice. They rushed through the reception hall, came out in the open and paused to look round. They were in the middle of a large field and a BMW 7 series car was parked about 100 feet away.

'come on let's move it' Nosa screamed. They made for the car as a deafening alarm began to roll. Before they could get to the car, they heard a blast of gun fire behind them.

'get down' Ayo shouted dragging Nosa to the ground. They hit the ground and looked back; through the tall grasses, they saw six guards running towards them.

'watch out Nosa, remember we are not dying today' Nosa rolled round on the ground and opened fire on his enemy. Two dropped dead while the rest kept coming. Ayo quickly brought out a grenade from his jacket; he removed the safety pin and held on to it for 'bout six seconds then threw it. The grenade exploded immediately it touched the ground killing the advancing guards. They smiled and gave themselves a high five. The car was now about thirty feet away, they stood up and ran towards the car but there were two guards waiting by the car; the guards opened fire on them. Ayo quickly duck behind a tree while Nosa dropped on the ground as a slug sang past his ear. The guards kept firing at Nosa direction and the slugs perforated his surroundings.

'kill them'? Nosa screamed

Ayo shot the two guards and waved at Nosa to get up. As they got to the car, Nosa threw his AK47 at the back seat and sat behind the wheel. Surprised the key was in the ignition, he thumped the starter and the engine came to life. They laughed out so loud and Ayo went round the car and got into the passenger seat. Nosa let out the clutch and the car sprang forward like a cheetah squealing and headed north.

'where are we going'? Ayo asked

'to the nearest town. Look don't you worry now okay, remember I studied the map and with the GPS in this car we can't be lost'. Ayo smiled but the smile vanished when he saw a chopper behind them.

'we've got a problem Nosa'

'what was that'? Nosa asked looking at the side mirror. He saw the chopper and they both stared at themselves for a moment. The chopper was now coming to rest on the BMW to force it to stop.

'use everything we've got on it' Nosa said and increased speed to 130km/hr. the road was dry and the dust was reducing the visibility of the pilot.

Ayo climbed to the back seat wind down the glass half way and poked his head out of the window but the dust from the road forced his head back. He brought out his .45 automatic, forced his head out and began to fire sporadically; the pilot screamed and the chopper changed course.

'I think I got the pilot'

'good did you see any other person in the chopper'?

'I think I sighted Bamidele , Bobbo and two other guys.

Nosa cursed under his breath. So Alhaji thinks Bamidele would scare us he thought; Nosa increased the speed to 170km/hr. although the road was dusty, he kept going at that speed.

'they're coming back'.

Nosa looked at the side mirror and could see the chopper coming with all its strength and with all its lights on. The chopper was now firing at them.

'I think we're lucky boy'

'and why is that' Nosa asked

'I think this car is bullet proof'

'and why did you think so'?

'their slugs are not penetrating the car'.

'alright but be careful how you stick your head out' Nosa said his eyes fixed on the road ahead.

The chopper went pass them and reversed. As it came towards them, Ayo brought out his AK47 and opened fire. The chopper came on strong and began to circle the car. Ayo quickly wind the glass up and Nosa began to maneuver the car. The chopper mounted the car and Nosa began to curse as the weight of the chopper slowed them down. They were now approaching a tarred road.

'let them have the grenade' Nosa said as they entered the tarred road. Ayo brought out the grenade and held it for some seconds; he wind down carefully and tossed it into the chopper. The chopper immediately left the car and swerved to the left. Ayo saw three people jump out and he smiled. His smile grew a mile wider when the chopper exploded then without warning; the car began to reduce speed.

'what's wrong" Ayo asked.

'am afraid we've ran out of fuel'. Nosa said looking at the dash board.

Ayo stiffened and looked at the dashboard. The fuel gauge was at zero. He cursed under his breath and looked back. They were about 6000 feet away from where the chopper exploded. The car came to a halt and they got out.

'well buddy, that was a great move, but we sure didn't think of this in our plans'. Nosa said.

Ayo sat on the tarred road and looked straight ahead.

'even if we walk from here, I don't care'

Nosa smiled and leaned on the car. It had happened like a dream or even in the movies; for them to beat Alhaji in his own game was something worth celebrating. But they knew there is no room for celebration yet until they get home. Alhaji will definitely send his men after them. After all they had all the weapons and means to do so. He looked at Ayo and jerked his head to the car.

'let's see what this car is made of'.

Without waiting for Ayo, he opened the door and began to search the car not knowing exactly what he was looking for. Ayo stood up and looked towards the place the chopper had come down. He could see three figures in the distance coming towards them. It was then he remembered three people had jumped out of the chopper before it went on fire.

'come here' Nosa was saying

Ayo turned round to face Nosa. Nosa was smiling and holding something in his hand.

'can see what your holding, what's that'? Ayo asked

'it's a binoculars, it could be useful you know'.

'we've got company' Ayo said pointing at the direction of the approaching assault men. Nosa stiffened and looked at the direction Ayo pointed to.

'ohhh not again'. He opened the back door, took his AK47 and swung it on his shoulders.

'allow me use the binoculars'. Nosa handed it to him and waited. Ayo looked into it and muttered something under his breath. Nosa snatched the binoculars from him and looked himself. He stiffened when he saw Bamidele , Bobbo and a guard. Bamidele was carrying a Mauser with a .45 automatic dug into his belt, bobbo carried a rifle with a twisted face and the guard was carrying an AK47. Nosa smiled, he knew by now, bobbo would be angry and would want their heads on a plate; but that is not going to happen he said to himself.

'that guard is new don't' you think Ayo'?

'am worried about Bamidele not Bobbo or the guard'

'well none of them scare me' Nosa said. He relaxed the binoculars and sat on the car bonnet.

'they are ready for war' he said.

Ayo looked round and said;

'we'll better hide inside the grass or else they will cut us in pieces'. Nosa went back to the car, brought out the remaining two grenades and removed the car keys. He looked around the car and went to the boot, opened it and saw a metal box.

'my gawd' he exclaimed; 'what have we here'. Ayo joined him and they both brought out the box; the box was very heavy and they set it down carefully.

Nosa cleaned the sweat on his face and said;

'I will be dammed if this is just an ordinary metal box'.

Ayo looked at the approaching assault team and turn to Nosa.

'we'll better stop this people first before we open that box'. Nosa looked up, they were about 500 feet away now.

'okay Ayo, let's go forward and attack them from there'. They grabbed their weapons and began to run towards the assault team with their heads bent very low.

'let's separate' Ayo said moving left. They dropped on the ground and waited; when their opponents were about forty-five feet away, they opened fire. The slugs from Nosa's AK47 scudded its way into Bobbo's lap; he squealed like a pig and dropped on the ground. Nosa smiled and looked through the binoculars; Bobbo was trying to tie the leg with a piece of cloth he had torn from his shirt. He searched through the grasses and saw Bamidele ; he was hiding behind a stump of tree, with the guard beside him. He crawled like a crocodile to the left and the guard opened fire on him but missed.

'I 've got bobbo' Nosa said coming to rest by Ayo

'is he dead'?

'no I think he'll live'.

'give me the binoculars'. Nosa handed it over to Ayo and he looked and saw Bamidele figure lurked behind a tree stump with the guard. He dropped the binoculars and brought out a grenade; he looked at Nosa who gave him a nod.

'it's better they die this way' Nosa said. Ayo removed the safety pin waited for some seconds and threw it to them but Bamidele saw it on time he shouted to the guard and rolled quickly away but the guard never made it. As he heard Bamidele shout he jumped up to run and the grenade exploded; he died instantly.

Nosa and Ayo looked up as they saw a chopper coming; they quickly crawled back towards the car and waited in the grasses. Nosa looked through the binoculars and saw Bamidele waving to the chopper, as the chopper came close he climbed into it and began to shout something to the pilot. The pilot circled round Bobbo, a hand came out; pulled him in and the chopper reversed and left. Ayo smiled and came to seat on the box.

'they gave up so easily' he said

'yeah but they will come back; and when they do, it will be heavy'.

They watched the chopper until it disappeared.

Alhaji sat behind his desk looking very furious but there were also traces of fear on his face. If those bastards he thought slip out of his hands then they will be blown. They would sure take the issue to the authorities and their cover would be blown. He cursed himself for being too liberal with them; he had thought they were harmless. He looked round him and grimaced. Everything stunk to him now. How the hell did they get the route of the building he reason. Alhaji knew there was no way they could have gotten out without the plan of the building. It must have been an inside job. But all his guards and friends were loyal to him; so who must have betrayed him. He opened his drawer and brought out a .45 colt automatic and checked it. The gun was loaded he grinned sheepishly and returned it to the drawer and left it open so he can reach it easily. He might not be safe anymore. A tap on the door interrupted his thoughts. He looked at the CCTV screen, it was blank. Slowly he pressed the button on his desk and the doors swung open. Lawani came inside and sat down opposite him.

'how far have you gone'? Alhaji snapped.

'nothing much. They got away with Bobbo's' car but Bamidele Bobbo and Dule are after them'.

Alhaji relaxed when he heard Bamidele name. He was sure Bamidele will handle them better than any other person.

'but there is a problem' Lawani started; the BMW is an armory itself'.

Alhaji jerked forward and placed his two hands on the desk.

'what was that you said, sorry I wasn't listening'.

Lawani leaned back on his chair taking his time. He knew it was a bad news Alhaji wouldn't like but he had to say it.

'the car is bullet proof and is carrying a steel box that contains two bazookas, one RPG, three double barrel guns, about six AK47s, three revolvers and thirty grenades'

Alhaji couldn't control himself anymore. He almost jumped out of his chair. He stared back at Lawani as if he just heard the voice of a spirit his eyes popping out with surprise; he just sat down there his mouth wide open like a church door.

Lawani looked away pretending not to see him. He stared at his hands but not really seeing them. Alhaji recovered from his shock and got up. He wandered aimlessly round the room and finally came to sit on the chair.

'with that at their disposal do you think we stand a chance'? he asked surprise his voice was quite.

'of….. of course we can. Come on Alhaji, It just the two of them but let's wait to hear from Bamidele '.

Alhaji looked at Lawani with cold eyes. The looked surprised him and made him shiver a bit.

'what's the matter'? he asked

'I think there escape was an inside job'. Lawani stared at him with mute amazement.

What makes you think so'? he demanded.

'those boys couldn't have left this building so easily without the building plan and details of the security. What about the CCTV? It's not working, something is wrong Lawani '.

Lawani 's eyes popped out. Since their prisoners escaped, he had not thought of that. He looked at Alhaji and shook his head.

'nobody would dare betray you, not even Bamidele . The stakes are too high for him am very sure of that'.

'then how did they get away so easily that they killed every patrol on duty. They seem to know every detail of the security arrangements'.

Lawani looked at him for a moment and got up.

'where are you going'?

Lawani paused near the door and looked back.

'let me check their rooms. I might find something'.

'alright but I want you here in five minutes'. As Lawani got out, Alhaji relaxed again in his chair. He began to wonder how those boys had escape with such skills. He had never known or had a clue that they were that good. He thought about the guards that were killed; while some were killed with knives and bullets others with bare hands. He was sure these boys must have undergone some sort of military training for them to be able to tackle his men so easily. He searched his brains for a way they could get them but he just couldn't think. Lawani's entering brought him back from his thoughts.

'yes, what did you find'?

'it's unbelievable Alhaji. I met Dauoda in Nosa's room with a broken neck and in Ayo's room; we fished out the plan and a map of Kaduna state. There was also a kit bag under the mattress.

'good heavens so it was Dauoda eh'?

'no am sure he was tortured for the Intel cause his hands and legs were tied and burnt'.

Alhaji was burning with fury. He stood up and sat down again. He clasped his hands as if to pray and leaned his head on them. The telephone rang and he picked it at first ring

'yes'.

'it's me Bamidele '

'did you get them'?

'am afraid no sir'.

'okayy come to my office'. Minutes later, Bamidele entered the office.

'sit down'. Alhaji said

'how far did you go'? Bamidele shook his head and sat down.

'they are both crazy. They got bobbo on his lap; shot the pilot, killed Dule and destroyed our chopper'.

He sat down and crossed his legs. Alhaji looked at Bamidele and bit his lower lip.

'what do you think of them'?

'I think they must be military or have had some kind of training or something. They are just crazy'.

'how did they destroy the chopper'? Lawani asked

'they tossed a grenade into the culprit'. Lawani stiffened.

'they must have opened the steel box' he said.

Alhaji closed his drawer and leaned forward.

'this matter is turning sour and I don't like the way it is going'.

He turned to Lawani.

'I want you to get Bisi for me dead or alive; I don't care how you do it. I want her here before evening tomorrow'.

Lawani said he will do just that and went out.

'as for you Bamidele , I don't care how you do it just get those boys back here for me to handle myself. I will want to see Ayo's face when he sees Bisi now go'.

Lawani went straight to his office and asked the secretary to get Bodde for him. After some minutes, Bodde came into his office and sat down.

'they said you want to see me'?

'yes. Send your best men after Bisi; tell them to bring her here whether, wounded or alive. Use force if necessary'. Bodde nodded his head and said;

'anything else'?

'we want her here as early as tomorrow'.

Dr. Chandler tap lightly on the door marked 'PRESIDENT', opened it and went inside. The office was lavishly big and it had several portraits of past presidents on the white wall at the left hand side of the office. There was a big desk that you could play snooker on with a desktop computer at the left hand side corner of the desk. The President was sitting on a lavishly built black leather chair with his hands resting on the arms of the chair. To his right was a set of brown chairs around a small glass table where he uses to relax with friends. To the left was a battery of polished cabinets, made from walnut wood and there was a giant toy plane hanging from the roof. There were four men siting with their backs to him facing the President. Chandler could recognize them even when their backs were turned to him. There was Mr. Chume, then the chief of defense staff, the chief of staff and the secretary to government. He walked straight to the table and took his seat next to Mr. Chume. Chandler dropped his brief case on the floor in between his legs and said.

'good evening Mr. President'.

'good evening' the President replied. He looked at the others and nodded to them.

'so how far did it go'? the President asked in a very calm voice

'it all went well. We've told the Nigerian government about the whole story and they have dispatch their men and resources to hunt after them'.

Chandler paused to open his brief case. He brought a letter and handed it over to the President.

'they were however not happy with us concerning our failure to verify from them before giving out the tanks'.

The President took the letter from him and opened it. He quickly read through and looked up.

'the Nigerian President is definitely not happy with the way things have gone and he took his time to convey such in a letter. Well mistakes have been made on our part and I think will have to live with that'.

'I guess you will have to call the Nigerian President yourselves so you two can talk this out'. Chume said

'I think you are right'. The President said

'I have another opinion'; chief of defense was saying.

The President looked at him and raised his eye brow.

'even though you call him, I think you should still write an official letter to him just for documentation'

'the COD's right' the SSG said to the President

'okay, so write a reply and let me see it before I make the call'. The president said handing the letter over to the SSG.

'and please gents, let's try not to make such a fool of ourselves again. Nigeria is not a country will can afford to have breathing on our backs'. The men in the room nodded in agreement and the president dismissed them.

CHAPTER THIRTEEN

Bisi and Ufan sat down at the reception of Chief Latif's office. The police officer behind the desk had told them to hold on for some time as the boss was busy. The girls relaxed and were admiring the office, whispering among themselves that they were not expecting to see a police office as furnished as what they were seeing there. The telephone on the table rang and the officer answered it, he replaced the receiver and asked them to go into the office. They stood up and went into the office;

'heelo ladies!' Mr. Latif called out as if they were miles away he stood up with huge smiles on his face and came around the desk to shake their hands.

'long time girls'.

Bisi and Ufan smiled back and took his hands. His hand was warm and soft and Ufan wondered why it was so. He waved them to sit and the ladies sat down.

'bout the guy you ladies told me the other time, we've got him'.

'who'? Ufan asked feigning surprise.

Latif looked at them for some time and grinned. He went to his chair and sat down.

'have you forgotten about Philip Emeka we talked about a week ago'?

'okay!' Bisi exclaimed 'what about him'?

'he turned himself in and has made a confessional statement'.

'well that's great!' Ufan said keeping her face expressionless.

'but there is something that bothers me about the two of you. You ladies talked about Emeka and two days later, he turned himself in; and the barman in the hotel said he saw two ladies meeting with him before we arrived'.

The chief paused, he stood up and walked to the table top fridge at the corner of the office and brought out three chilled cans of malt. He served the ladies, opened his own and sat down again; then he took a sip and continued.

'that same day, Mr. Ola, the chairman of Nigerian union of scientist phoned me and complained about both of you. He thinks you girls are in some sort of trouble. He also complained that Ayo and Nosa had been sort of missing but you two are insisting they have gone on vacations.'

He waited for the talk to sink into them and drank half of the drink.

'I thought about these issues and placed two officers to monitor you two. And so far, reports before me says that you girls applied for leave which you got but you girls seems to be running up and down chasing something'.

He stopped talking and leaned forward; Bisi and Ufan were staring at him now. He grinned and leaned back on his seat.

'now would you please tell me what is going on? I've always promise to be of help to you; how do you want me to say it again'?

Bisi turned her calm eyes on the chief. So the car they've seen at the museum was one of the chief's. she smiled and dropped her hand bag on the floor.

'that's why we are here. We've come to tell you something you might think incredible.'

'wait' the chief said holding out his hand. 'before you say anything, let me call in my personal assistant'.

He raised the telephone receiver and dialed three digits.

'yes chief'

'I want you up here now'. He dropped the receiver and waited. The room was silent and the ladies opened their cans and began to drink. After a minute or so, the door opened and Jegbefo stepped in and closed the door.

'hey Jeg!' Bisi shouted jumping up from her chair; she hugged him passionately with her drink in her right hand.

'when did you come'?

'last night' he said smiling. He held on to her left hand.

'meet my friend Ufan'. Ufan stood up and shook him warmly.

'Bisi has talked so much about you'

'really' Jeg said looking at Bisi.

Chief Latif watched with keen interest and allowed them to finish.

'you said you need me chief'?

'yes put on the light and sit down, the ladies have something for us'.

Jeg switch on the light behind the chief, sat down next to Bisi and clasped his hand on his lap like a school boy and waited.

'before we start, we'll like to say that this issue is top secret and that we will like to be involved no matter how life threatening it is'.

Chief Latif and Jeg sat up with their ears wide open. This was not going to be an ordinary routine case.

'i…i..i… don't think I have the power to bring you into a case we have not heard'.

Bisi looked at Ufan who shook her head quietly.

'you need to give us your word on this chief, we are serious'.

Jeg took a sharp look at the chief and scratched his head

'alright' the chief said; 'we'll count you in'.

'good' Bisi said and started her story. She started from the day she was almost kidnapped before Jeg recused her, she told them of their encounter with Obakpolor and Emeka. She also told them on how they've tried not to allow anyone to know and ended up with the letter from Ayo and Nosa's disappearance. She didn't hold back anything; when she finished, she took the last of her drink and raised her hands up.

'so, that's it' she said.

Latif sat still for some minutes. He just couldn't believe all what he has just heard. He glanced at Jeg and saw he too was in shock at the story. So many security issues had been happening in his state he thought. With steady hands, he picked up his can malt and emptied the remaining contents inside his mouth; he dropped the empty can on the desk and waited.

'you mean' the chief started 'that this kind of info was with you ladies and you kept it to yourselves? What exactly was your plan?

'we are sorry chief. I think we wanted to gather enough evidence before we came forward. It seemed to us initially that they were mere routine kidnappers we hear of in the dailies'.

Chief Latif opened his drawer and brought out a bottle of whiskey and a glass. He poured himself a drink, gulped it and poured another. He looked across the desk at Bisi and Ufan; they were very calm and waiting for his reaction. He looked at Jeg, he was tapping his right leg on the floor.

'maybe you girls don't know the gravity of this matter. This issue is beyond my pay grade and it's going up to the presidency. I have no power to dictate in an issue of this magnitude; we all need to appear before the President'.

'we're aware of this sir'. Bisi said her voice very calm. Jeg held her hand, patted it and said.

'it's good you two came forward with this. This issue looks complex and it might be a hell of a time locating these people but the government will take it from here now'.

The chief looked at Bisi directly and said'

'what did you say was their name'?

'Amamadas or so that was the name Ayo called them in his letter'.

'can I have the letter'? Chief Latif said stretching his hands. Bisi opened her hand bag and brought out the letter; she stood up and handed it over to the chief who collected it carefully and went through it. When he was through, he picked up the receiver and dialed a number. Bisi went back to her chair and sat down.

'come up here now'. He dropped the receiver carefully but his hand was still on it; he was very deep in thoughts, raking his brains.

'we'll keep this letter for you till we hand it over to the Federal authorities but first, I'll like to know what it's made of'.

The door opened and a fat police officer came in. Ufan looked at her and hid a grin. The blouse of the officer will be enough for her to sew a blouse and a skirt she thought. Jeg caught her and she smiled. The officer closed the door carefully, saluted the chief and greeted the girls generally; she then tiptoed to the chief's desk.

'send it to the lab' Latif said handling the letter to her. 'this is top secret, so stand by them until they finish with it and bring it back here'.

'yes chief, when do you want it'? she asked

'yesterday'.

She nodded her head and tiptoed again out of the office.

'ladies' the chief called out; I was right in putting two officers on you but right now, I will withdraw them and replace them with Jeg. I can see you girls are no longer safe at all'.

Bisi and Ufan whispered something for a moment.

'okay chief, that's fine with us' Bisi said.

'for a moment I thought you were going to protest that again'. The chief said. The girls laughed.

'how are we sure you will not go to the Presidency without bringing us in'? Ufan asked.

'don't worry' Jeg said 'the Presidency would want to see you two. You can be sure of that'.

'okay ladies, you'll hear from us soon'.

Bisi and Ufan thanked him and got up. Jeg joined them as they got to the door. He opened for them and as they went out, he paused by the door frame and turned to the chief;

'have you heard anything from Bamidele '?

'no, since the past three months now, I have not heard a word from him'.

'poor boy' Jeg said; 'am sure his sister's disappearance is what is driving him up and down. But how far have you gone with the case'?

Chief Latif leaned back on his chair and shook his head.

'not a dam lead Jeg. We can't even locate him'.

'well you know Dele, he decided to take up the case himself. See you later sir'.

He raced down the staircase and joined the girls.

'where are you two going now'?

'to the house'. Ufan said

Jeg adjusted his tie and opened the front glass door for them and stepped back. They got out and entered Ufan's Benz E300 and drove towards the gate. Jeg waited inside the office and watched them from the glass door then he saw a black Range rover sport come out from behind a parked utility van and drove after the Benz E300. He smiled as he watched the car heading for the gate. He raced to the reception and told him to call the security at the gate to stop the Black Range rover. Jeg raced out of the reception office and began running towards the SUV cautiously with his .45 automatic on hand. The E300 had just driven past the gates and the securities were now stopping the Range rover, the gate was locked. Jeg saw the security asking the driver to step out of the vehicle; the driver hesitated and put the Range rover in reverse. The two officers at the security post immediately opened fire with their .38 police special, but the vehicle kept reversing, Jeg was now almost at its tail. He could see three men inside. The Range rover stopped and began to drive forward with squealing tires heading for the gates. Jeg could tell that they were attempting to run the SUV through the gate. The firing from the security post had perforated the SUV. The men were returning the fire now; the whole station was agog with gun fire.

'we want them alive….. we want them alive'. Jeg was shouting.

He knelt down on the gravel, took an aim and the .45 automatic came alive. The bullet hit the driver at the back of the head as the SUV went crashing at the gates. The gates though seriously damaged, held it. There was airbag all over inside the range rover. Jeg stood up and raced to the vehicle, the men had stop firing. He approached the vehicle with caution; the back door of the passenger side opened and a man jumped out with Mauser in his hand, Jeg could see that he was slightly injured. He quickly attacked him and hit the gun out of his hand as the security crowded the gun man, put him down and handcuffed his hands behind him. The other guy at the front sit was badly injured with bullet holes and part of his head was riddled with the scattered glass.

'call an ambulance.... Call an ambulance'; Jeg heard the chief shouting behind him. He looked back and saw chief Latif racing towards him; he wondered why the chief always like to be part of an action even at his level.

'but chief you could have stayed back in your office'; he was saying.

The chief ignored him. The two officers holstered their weapons and heaved the gunman to his feet;

'what gut! take him in and lock down the entire building no one goes out' the chief said. Jeg's phone rang and he quickly picked it.

'yes' he said

'we think a car is after us'. Bisi was shouting on the phone.

'where are you'

'we are along Sapele road but we're now going through the roundabout by Ikpokan junction'.

'what type of car is it'?

'it's a black Toyota Tundra'.

'good, drive towards the meg filling station here, I will meet you there'.

'the ladies are still being chased'

He told the chief. Before the chief could reply him, Jeg took off. He quickly dash through the small gate out of the premises. There was a dispatched motor bike parked outside, the firing had made the road deserted and Jeg could see about seven men from the State Security Service building, opposite the police headquarters running towards them armed to the teeth. He climbed the bike and zoomed off. As he got to the intersecting junction, he jumped of the bike, ran to the middle of the road and waited. The traffic was very light, the shootings heard in the police headquarters must have scared motorist off the road. He could see the E300 coming at top speed; the Tundra hit a Honda civic car in front of it and the car smashed into a pharmacy shop. The SUV came on strong and began to use its size to press the Benz to the pillars portioning the road. Ufan was trying to keep the car steady as she pushed back on the SUV but the Tundra seems to be gaining the upper hand. The side mirror of the E300 broke off as the side of the car was being pressed to the pillars. Metal and concrete were struggling and it was taking a toll on the Benz but Ufan kept coming toward Jeg. As both vehicles came close, he raised his .45 automatic, aimed at the driver of the Tundra and fired thrice. The SUV vied of the E300 and came towards him. He fired several shots again and jumped off the road just in time as the Tundra climbed the walk way and rammed into Eatery shop on its right. The impact of the crash was deafening and it made People to rush out of the eatery. Ufan swung the battered E300 to the left to face the road to the police headquarters and stopped the car. Jeg quickly reloaded and raced to the SUV, he raised his gun as he approached the vehicle cautiously. The back doors opened and two men came out, one that was badly injured fell on the ground bleeding; the other was carrying an AK47. On sighting the AK, Jeg hit the ground as the gunman opened fire. He rolled on the ground thrice and shot him on the chest but the gunman kept firing until he hit the ground. Jeg looked round, the place was deserted; from the corner of his eyes, he saw Ufan and Bisi running towards him. He tried to stand but he couldn't feel his left, he rolled over and tried to sit down still holding on to his .45 automatic. Bisi and Ufan rushed to him and held him up.

'you're a brave cop'. Bisi said

'yes, the best I've ever seen'. Ufan was saying.

He smiled and looked at his leg. It was bleeding; they looked up when they heard cars approaching, it was Chief Latif and a team of police men in company of some SSS men. The chief jumped out of the car and rushed to Jeg as the policemen sealed off the entire area. Jeg forced a grin at the chief who patted his head. The chief examined the leg and smiled.

'you're lucky'. He said 'the bullet missed your bone'. Jeg handed over his gun to the Chief as two officers took him from the girls and helped him into the Police car and the driver drove off immediately.

'searched the van'. The chief told the two officers standing by him. They cautiously approached the SUV and searched it. Ufan and Bisi stood by the chief and watched. The SSS men entered the eatery and began to comb the entire area. The driver was very dead from the bullet wounds and the other man in front was also dead. Chief Latif squatted beside the bleeding gunman on the ground, he looked at him critically; this was Alhaji Abudu's personal body guard he thought. He was sure of it cos' they've met few times at functions; there was a hole in his chest and his right hand was badly riddled probably from the shattered glass. Latif was sure that the man would die of the wounds. He was trying to say something so the chief bent very low to hear him.

'you are all dead men' the man whispered

Chief Latif smiled and whispered back to him.

'no, you are wrong, you and Alhaji Abudu are dead already'.

He smiled again when he saw the surprise on the man's face. The gunman died in his surprise. Chief Latif closed his eyes and looked round; the SSS men were coming out of the eatery with the manager, staff and customers. The chief could see the fear and surprise on their faces.

'sorry for the trouble, pain and damages this has caused you'. The chief said. 'my boys has contained the situation and it's okay now. Just estimate your damages and bring it to the office, the government will take of it okay'?

The manager nodded and mumbled something. The chief looked at the SSS men and raised his eyebrow.

'it's all clear'. The team leader said

Crowds were now gathering and the police had set up a barricade round the scene. The Chief looked round the crowd, he sighted a reporter and her cameraman trying to go through the police; he then turned to Bisi and Ufan;

'how are you ladies'?

'we are fine chief' they chorused.

'can you see this issue is getting uglier by the day'?

The ladies nodded.

'that your car' the chief started pointing to the E300, will be remanded in the office for a while. Hope you girls won't protest that'.

'no we won't. Ufan said.

'good'.

The chief gave others to his men and asked a tall slim officer to take charge of the scene. He thanked the SSS men for their support as they began to leave and asked another officer to take Ufan and Bisi home. The Chief straightened his uniform, cleared his throat and walked towards the reporter, at least he would have to tell her something. He wasn't going to allow them to speculate any news under his watch.

CHAPTER FOURTEEN

Bamidele switched on the radio and lied back on the bed again. He listened to the radio for some minutes and lowered the volume. He was angry now; he looked round the room and hissed. It was now time for him to carry out his plans. His mind went back to four months earlier when Alhaji had ordered the kidnapping of Pamela his sister while on vacation somewhere in Lagos. Alhaji had taken her to get at Bamidele and had asked him to work for him for some time before the sister is returned to him. It was very difficult for him to contact his partner Jegbefo as Lawani had planted a microchip inside him. His phones and emails were tapped and he was monitored like a criminal. Since he had no choice, he was compelled to work for Alhaji but up till now, Alhaji had not kept his own side of the bargain. At least he had played a role of loyalty to the point of attracting hatred from Ayo and Nosa yet his sister had still not been released to him.

Bamidele got up. He went to the cabinet, poured himself a drink, then carried the whiskey and glass back to the bed and sat down. Alhaji had made him a smoker and he was sure his pretense had paid off very well. He was now like an undercover agent only in his case; they were watching his next move like a chess player. Bamidele knew that as a former military general in the Nigerian army, Lawani was good and could read most of his moves like an Olympic medalist in chess but he was smarter and had always played the fool and that had helped him get the location of his sister. He was not surprised when he learnt Pamela was being kept in Lawani's apartment and was guarded by three guards. He was confident he can handle Lawani when the time comes; since he leaked information to Paul and Kola in his last trip to Bamako, things were happening too fast now and he knew Lawani and Alhaji would have begun to be suspicious of him. But he was certain that they had not known his role in the escape of Ayo and Nosa. He knew the boys were planning an escape and so he had disabled the CCTV in the corridor and on the surface. He had also parked Bobbo's car outside with some food stuff to ease their escape. But what Ayo and Nosa did not know is that they were his seniors in the Nigerian Defense Academy and he knows them very well as they had graduated three years ahead of him. Bamidele was also aware of how the boys had decided to become civilians after their peace keeping mission in the Liberia civil war. Though he had run into them on two occasions in the state, he had kept a distance from them since he was made to serve in the Nigerian police as an undercover agent for the directorate of military intelligence. He took his drink in a gulp and poured another one this time the glass was almost half full. Although his movement within the building was sort of free, he was aware that Lawani had given a directive to all the guards to watch him. No one was his friend and he wasn't prepared to make any his friend either. The intercom in the room interrupted his thoughts. He stood up and went to pick up the phone.

'yes'.

'it's me Yerima. We are ready for takeoff'.

'okay, I'll be with you guys in a jiffy'. Bamidele replaced the receiver on the cradle and emptied the drink in his mouth. He grimaced and waited a bit for the drink to take effect.

'alright' he said to himself; 'it's time for me to start my trouble'. He set the glass on the table at the middle of the room, opened the door and stepped out. He ran through the corridor and took the elevator to the top floor. The chopper was waiting and it took off as he climbed into it. Yerima was at the front sit with the pilot. He was carrying a Mauser striped to his hip; the pilot had two smoke gas cans strapped to his hip and there were four other gunmen with machine guns. Bamidele nodded to them and causally looked round the chopper; his instincts was telling him that for Alhaji to send Yerima one of his personal body guard to head the search team, his suspicions of the organization not trusting him had been confirmed. The chopper raced through the hot sun and when it approached the area they last encountered Ayo and

Nosa, it came down cautiously and began to circle the area after some time, the pilot shook his head and said;

'not a sign of them'.

Yerima leaned out and searched the ground thoroughly.

'take her down a little' he said patting his right hand down in the air. As the chopper lost height, they heard a burst of gun fire and Yerima screamed as the slugs perforated his right arm. The gunmen began to shot sporadically towards were they had heard the shootings from. In the confusion, the pilot tilted the chopper to climb and Yerima fell off but he was quick to hold on to the landing gear.

'help me'! he yelled out at Bamidele. Dele grabbed his hand as the chopper gained height; from the corner of his eyes, he watched to see if the others were looking at him but they were more occupied in returning the fire. Satisfied they were not watching him, he let go of Yerima. He screamed as he danced in the air before hitting the ground.

'those bastards'. Bamidele was saying he looked at the pilot and shouted at him to take the chopper down. The chopper came down about 100 feet from the spot of gunfire and the pilot landed it carefully.

'wait here and keep the engine running' Bamidele said. He turned to the others;

'okay boys you saw what they did to Yerima, this is it, let's go get some blood'.

They jumped out of the chopper and dropped on the ground.

'two of you go to the right and the rest stay with me. We'll circle them and box them in'

Bamidele said. When the rest two were out of sight, Bamidele caught sight of Ayo lying flat on his belly with a machine gun hiding in the grasses to his right.

'both of you go that way'. He said pointing to Ayo's direction. The gunmen began to crawl towards Ayo. Before they could get half way, Ayo opened fire and one of them went limp. The other stop, he caught a glimpse of Ayo and rolled over to the left. As he raised his gun to fire Ayo, Bamidele shot him at the back of his head. Ayo looked up and saw Bamidele; Bamidele could see the shock in his eyes. He grinned at Ayo and threw his Mauser at him. Ayo almost stood up to run thinking it was a grenade but when he saw it was a gun, he caught it and crawled back. Bamidele stood up and raced back to the chopper; he knew Ayo and Nosa would take care of the other two gunmen. He got in front and shouted at the pilot to take off. When the chopper had gained about two thousand feet, Dele brought out a .45 colt automatic from his holster and shot the pilot twice on the head. As the pilot fell forward on the controls, Dele removed the smoke cans from him and pushed him off the chopper; he put the cans inside his jacket and quickly took over controls. He looked round the chopper, there was a machine gun; he picked it up and sprayed few shots inside the chopper.

It was time for him to make trouble he thought. He would have to get back as quickly as he can, get his sister and come for Nosa and Ayo. He knew he couldn't approach them without a good reason as they will cut him in pieces. Alhaji and Lawani would be waiting for results and he was ready to give them a shocker. He rode the chopper confidently because he knew that most of the foot soldiers had been sent to strategic locations and there were only a handful of guards in the headquarters now. As he approached the Amamadas headquarters hideout, he saw two guards standing at the landing area of the chopper. He hid a grin as he saw the surprise on their faces seeing him alone inside the chopper. He cautiously landed the chopper and left the engine running. He was aware that the disabled CCTV had not been fixed yet because of the serious damage to it. Alhaji would have to fly in an expert to fix the cameras and with the situation of things as it stands now, that would not be immediate. From the corner of his eyes, he could see that one of the guards had drawn his .45 automatic as he stepped out of the chopper. He pretended to miss his step and the guard in front with the gun reached out to him to hold him. Bamidele grabbed his right hand and broke it. The guard screamed with agonizing pain as the gun fell from his hand. Dele hit him at the back of his head and he fell face down. The other guard rushed him and launched a punch at Bamidele; though he saw the punch coming, it hit his neck before he could avoid it. The punch sent Dele staggering backwards; Dele regained his balance and in a swift move, turned around with a karate kick. It hit the guard on his jaw and blood gathered in his mouth. The guard paused for a while and spat the blood on the ground; a tooth fell off. He cleaned his mouth and came forward but this time Dele was ready. He went round him in a swift motion and locked his neck in his hands. The man struggled vigorously swinging his hands hopelessly in the air as Bamidele applied pressure. After some seconds or so, he went limp and Dele allowed him to hit the ground. He looked round, picked up the .45 and took the elevator. So Alhaji and Lawani have already given the order to detain him he thought. He knew they will be waiting for him downstairs as well but he will give them hell; he brought out a silencer from his jacket, screwed it to the gun and climbed up the elevator holding on to the hook on the roof. He waited for the doors to open. As the doors opened, there were sporadic gun fire from the corridor but when the guards did not see anyone in the elevator, they stopped. As one of them entered the elevator cautiously, Dele dropped from the roof and held on to his neck with his left hand while pointing the .45 on the head.

'drop your guns' he said to the other two that were standing with their mouths opened. They dropped their guns; Bamidele stepped out of the elevator and quickly looked round. They were alone in the corridor. He shot them both while holding on to the one with him.

'where is Lawani '? he asked pushing him forward.

'i…i.. don't know'.

Bamidele shot him on his thigh through the bone and pressed the silencer on the spot. He let out a groaning pain and raised his hands up.

'i…ll tell you please, please stop…. stop'.

'okay where'?

'he's waiting for you in his apartment'

'and Alhaji'?

'he has gone into the bunker'.

Bamidele paused for a while as if considering what to do. The man was sobbing badly and he could here footsteps approaching. He held on to the guard as the footsteps got louder. Two gunmen came round the bend and opened fire on sighting Bamidele. He used the guard as a shield as they sprayed the guard nonstop. He let the man go and dropped on the ground shooting them as he hit the floor. The corridor was quite for a while. Dele got up and opened the door to his left. There was a staircase. He took it down at random and came to a door facing the stairs. He opened it gently, the door was locked. He moved back a bit, hit it and dived on the lobby floor. As the door burst open, a trail of gunfire filled the air. Dele released the safety pin from the smoke gas and threw them into the room. He rolled away from the door and waited; a round of gun fire erupted again. Later he heard people coughing uncontrollably. He stood up and came near the door frame and waited; three men ran out coughing, he's .45 hissed thrice and they dropped on the ground.

'so this is how you want it ehh'?

It was Lawani. He was coughing too. Bamidele could hear Pamela coughing uncontrollably but there was nothing he could do about that. She would probably pass out or she would have to hold on for some time.

'you will never leave here alive Bamidele , you'll see'.

Bamidele was very quiet. Pamela had stopped coughing. The smoke was very tick now and Lawani began shooting sporadically. Bamidele went on all four and began to crawl into the room. He held on to his breath and through the smoke could see Pamela tied to a chair, she had passed out and Lawani was standing behind her. But Lawani was dazed by the smoke and could not see very well. Too much laxity and indulgence had softened Lawani Bamidele thought. He crawled up to Lawani and stood up. Lawani had run out of cartridge now and he began to curse. Bamidele hit him on his fore head and that knocked him out as he fell on the ground. He opened the drawer took out the three files, shoved it into the jacket and zipped it. He then brought out Lawani 's lap top. Dele smashed it on the ground and used his shoe to finish the work; he bent down and removed the hard drive from the wreck, shoved it into his back pocket and quickly untied Pamela. He carried her on his shoulder. He would have to leave before the whole place come alive with Alhaji's men.

Bamidele came through the door cautiously and peeped at the staircase; it was quite. He bent down and picked up an AK47 from one of the dead guards and began to climb the staircase cautiously. When he got to the door, he opened it and peeped. Surprised the corridor was empty; he stepped out carefully and raced to the elevator. As he pressed the button, he held footsteps behind. He swung round and but didn't see anyone. As he stepped into the elevator, he held someone screaming at him. He turned to see four guards running towards him, he opened fire and could see one drop as the doors closed. He dropped Pamela at the corner of the elevator and balanced the AK47 in his hand. He was ready for anything that would be waiting at the top floor. The doors swung opened and he was surprised that no one was there. He poked out his head but there was no one in the reception hall. Bamidele carried the sister again, raced through the hall and came out in the open cautiously. The chopper was still there the way he left it. He heaved Pamela in the front, belt her up and got behind the controls. As he took off, he heard gun fire below. The chopper quickly gained height and he headed north. He would have to get Ayo and Nosa as the chopper is their best bet to escape. He knew he would have a lot of explanation to do but with the sister by his side, it would be easier. Pamela sneezed twice and opened her eyes; they were a little bit blurred. He stretched out his right hand and touched her face; she looked at him and smiled when she recognized him. She was a beauty to behold but she was too weak to speak.

'relax my dear' he said; 'we'll soon be home'

He gave the chopper more speed and Pamela closed her eyes again.

CHAPTER FIFTEEN

'it seems as if that guy has gone crazy'. Ayo was saying.

'who'? Nosa asked

'Bamidele shot his own man and threw his gun at me'.

Nosa stared at Ayo and shook his head

'don't you think I'll swallow that'.

'it's true. Here is his gun. He was even smiling at me'. Nosa's eyes popped out when he saw the Mauser. That was Bamidele 's favourite weapon.

'how and why will he do that'? Nosa asked.

Ayo examined the gun. It was loaded they looked at each other in surprise. Then they looked at the chopper that was now in faint distance.

'how did this happen'? Nosa asked again

'Search me, all I can remember is that I shot one of the men coming my way and he shot the other one when he tried to shot at me'. Nosa looked at Ayo and collected the Mauser from him. He looked at it over and over again trying to think of something.

'let's go back to our hide out'. he manage to say.

They made their way back to their hideout that was about two thousand hundred feet away. They had pushed the car into the cover of some tall grasses and it was a perfect cover except from a chopper circling the area. As they got to the BMW, Nosa opened the boot and dropped the Mauser inside the steel box. They were sort of trapped in the environment without mobility he thought. If they attempt to go on foot, it would be easy to catch them; their plans were to hijack the chopper and fly out of the vicinity; but they were also aware that Alhaji would not allow them leave to tell their story.

'do you think he's trying to deceive us'? Ayo interrupted his thought. Nosa said he had no idea and switched the topic.

'it was stupid of me to have left the map behind'. He said mumbling a curse.

'come on, don't blame yourself now; let's be patient and wait for that chopper. that is our only hope right now'.

'you're right Ayo, but waiting here too long is a high risk. That we've survived this long doesn't mean it will remain like this for long'.

'I know what you are thinking. At least our military skills has survived us this far. I know Alhaji would want us for dinner but he would have to work very hard for that. We'll come out fine Nosa, trust me'.

Just then, they heard the sound of an approaching chopper in the distance; they looked at each other.

'here we go again' Ayo said grabbing an AK47 from the boot. He quickly packed about three grenades into his jacket and watched Nosa do the same.

'this is it Nosa, this is our ride home'.

Bisi and Ufan were in the living room watching the television when Bisi's cell phone rang.

'I'll get it' Ufan said. She got up and picked the phone from the top of the dining table. She looked at the name of the caller and smiled

'hello chief' she said.

'the President wants both of you; so get dressed. We'll be there in ten minutes'.

'alright chief, we'll be waiting' Ufan was excited and she couldn't hide it.

'the chief is on his way here to pick us to Aso rock. We have ten minutes Bisi'.

Bisi jumped up from the sofa and ran into her room. Ufan joined her and some minutes later, they were outside waiting. The sound of an approaching chopper polluted the skies as it made people in the street to start looking up.

The eight mobile police officers stationed around Bisi's apartment covered the two ends of the 15th street of the BDPA estate, each carrying an AK47 and a .38 police special strapped to their hips. The chopper came down slowly and landed close to Bisi's gate. Jegbefo opened the door as the ladies ran out and climbed in.

'Jeg'! Bisi screamed. He smiled and closed the door and the chopper took off. Bisi looked at Jeg and gave him a light hug.

'thank God you're okay'. she said

'how is the leg now'? Ufan asked

'it fine though it hurts a bit but am fine thank you'.

'well……well ……well' the chief started clearing his throat. 'hope you girls are ready for questions'? he said

Ufan nodded her head.

'of.. course' she said. Jeg opened a rucksack and brought out a file.

'I wrote down all you said, just in case they want your statement in writing. You can go through it'.

'thank you' Bisi said collecting the file. She went through the write up and finally nodded her heard. She brought out a pen, signed it and gave the file back to Jeg then turned to the chief.

'did you tell them that Ufan and I are on this issue to the end'?

'I did but the President will see you first before deciding on that'. They remained silent for the rest of the journey. The chopper finally got to Abuja; it circled in the air for some time until the pilot got clearance to land the chopper inside the Aso Rock Villa Helipad. The chopper came down slowly under the watchful eyes of stern looking security operatives armed to their teeth. There were two SSS operatives waiting by the helipad; the chief got out first and nodded to the SSS that saluted him. Jeg got out and the ladies followed. The security operatives then led the way into the villa. They took them through a corridor screed with white paint and decorated with paintings and portraits of past Nigerian leaders. The corridor brought them to a large reception hall. The hall was luxuriously furnished with polished wooden sofas and leather chairs. The walls were lined with polished plywood and there was a large desk with a fat man sitting behind it; he was eating sharwama with a bottle of Pepsi. He looked up as Chief Latif and his entourage entered the hall, nodded to them and went back to his menu. He still had one more wrap of sharwama to go and he was not going to allow anyone to disturb him. Bisi and Ufan looked round; they could count about eight SSS men standing at different point in the hall. There were also about six men and eight women in different traditional attires inside the hall sitting down and discussing in hush tones. Politicians no doubt Bisi thought. They would definitely be waiting to see the President. They looked up when they entered and their discussion stopped. One of the men sitting down seems to know chief Latif. He raised his hands to greet him but the chief just nodded and looked away.

'wait here'. One of the SSS men said. He crossed the hall and went through a glass door into a room; some minutes later, he came out and said to the chief;

'you people can go in now'. The people sitting down stared after them in mute amazement. They began to wonder among themselves how come they that have been there were not considered first to see the President. Chief Latif took the lead as they made their way quietly through the large hall; there was a tall heavily built security man at the end of the hall standing by a curved glass door. He looked well fed with his round face and broad shoulders. He made them pass through the glass door in single file and a ray of light pass through them. The door led them to a smaller reception hall; there was a lady of Bisi size sitting behind a desk with a battery of computers and its accessories. She would be in her mid- forties but her makeup was doing a very good job as one would think she was in her mid-thirties. This must be the President's secretary Ufan thought; the secretary was chewing gum and busy with her system. She looked up as they approached her desk and stood up; the secretary smiled at them and Bisi thought the smile was genuine.

'he is waiting for you, go right inside'. She said.

Chief Latif tapped the door lightly and opened it. The office was as big as a badminton court and was something else; the President was sitting behind a large brown polished desk big enough to play table tennis on. He had pictures of his wife and children in small portraits frame on the desk and a large portrait of the Nigerian coat of arms was hung on the wall behind him. There were six large brown chairs made of hippopotamus skin lined up in front of the large desk. To the president's right, were three settees of lemon and orange chairs circling a triangular glass table. To his left were three small purple sofas close to a huge black vase. A cabinet was standing at end of the office and it was slightly opened. The wall painting was milk and orange demarcated at the middle with white. The white and orange pop ceiling was smooth throughout but lined with flowered images at the edges. Then there was the green white green rug that spread from one end of the office to the other with the Nigeria coat of arms embedded at the center of the office.

'good evening Mr. President' Latif said bowing a bit as he entered the room.

'good evening' the President replied. 'are these the ladies'?

'yes Mr. President'. The President jerked his head to the right and studied them carefully.

'where you not the engineer that designed the General hospital that was funded by the world bank'? the President asked pointing at Bisi.

'yes I am Mr. President'.

'and you're that engineer that is among the team of engineers in charge of the turn round maintenance of our Kaduna refinery'?

'yyyou are right Mr. President'. Ufan stammered.

'please sit down'. the President said. He touched the button on his desk and spoke into it.

'send in the national security adviser and the defense minister now'. Bisi was the first to sit down; Ufan followed and the chief and Jeg sat down. Jeg causally looked round the office and studied the portraits on the wall. This office was something he thought, he doubted if the President could find comfort and warmth from the task and headaches of piloting a nation like Nigeria inside the office. He studied the President that was looking stressed and agitated. When he newly took over the saddle of leadership few years back, his hairs were still very black but it was not so anymore as the hairs where visibly turning white now. Becoming a national leader was tough he thought. Handling issues of security in the Edo state police command alone was a mind boggling task but for the Presidency, that was something else. The entrance of the NSA boss and the defense minister interrupted Jegbefo's thought.

'our friends are here' the President said. The men came in quietly and shut the door. The defense minister sat down and crossed his legs; he was putting on white fitted brocade attire with black shoes. The national security adviser came forward and dropped his briefcase on the desk. He was a well-respected retired army general with medals to his credit. His huge size was nothing to him as he carried himself with gait and pride. He was putting on a brown suit with brown shoes to match. He opened the briefcase and brought out a tape recorder and a brown envelop. Bisi and Ufan watched him quietly; although they were happy to be with the President of the Federal Republic of Nigeria, they had to admit that they were there for a serious purpose. This was a case of national security and it was obvious that the Presidency was playing it quietly since they can't ascertain those involved in the scheme yet. NSA switched on the tape; the girls sat up as Bisi's voice came up. Bisi took a sharp look at Latif who had been quiet all the while and he smiled. So he was recording in his office.

'are you surprised'? the President asked her

She shook her head nervously. The tape played on still the story was finished. The NSA stopped the tape and brought out Ayo's letter from the brown envelop.

'this is what the ladies informed chief Latif before one of the gunmen was apprehended right inside the Edo state police headquarters'.

'what guts! where is he now'. The President asked.

'in our custody Mr. President; he was transferred to us yesterday and has made some interesting confessions'.

'what did he say'? the President demanded

'you will not like it Mr. President' the NSA said.

'well, try me'.

The defense minister leaned forward in his chair and looking directly at the President, he said as if in a whisper;

'the master mind of all these is Alhaji Abudu Mali. He is trying to create chaos in the country by first creating diversionary bombings to incite groups and tribes against each other which would then encourage Islamic extremists and militants to unleash terror in the country'.

The President stared back at the Minister as if he had heard from a ghost. He turned his gaze to the NSA and then to Latif and his entourage.

'are you in sane'? he barked at the Minister. 'How can you say a thing like that? That man has benefitted immensely from this government in terms of tax exceptions and contracts running into billions. What does he stand to gain'?

The minister leaned back in his chair and allowed the President to absolve what he has just said. He knew the President would be shocked at the news hence they have held back the information till now.

'well, answer me'. The President said quietly. The words of the minister were now sinking in gradually. He knew the minster couldn't lie to him on such a critical national issue. They had known way back from their youth up till now and he had made him the minister of defense to watch his back for him.

'Mr. President', the minister continued; 'Alhaji Abudu has been an arms dealer way back during the civil war. He sold arms to the rebels then and he had been fingered in the Angola, Liberia, Sudan, and Sierra Leone wars.'

'how is that so? I mean how come I don't know about that?' the President said staring at the NSA.

'the minister is right Mr. President'. the NSA was saying trying to evade the question.

'if you recall, the intelligence the Togolese government provided, led us to Alhaji Abudu's hotel in Yola. But somehow, we couldn't get any concrete prove to effect an arrest; but with the confessional statement from the gunman, all is now set'.

'what do you mean by that'? the President asked.

The national security adviser nodded to the defense minister and sat down.

'we've assembled three tactical teams for a covert operation into their hideout. As we speak sir, the team is about ten kilometers away from their hideout and has set up a perimeter. The air force is providing air support and has sealed off the entire area. They're just waiting for a go sir'.

The room became as silent as a grave yard. Bisi and Ufan were frozen on their seats with their mouths opened. The President looked at them and stood up. He was shocked at the development. He paced round the office and came to rest by the glass window frame at the end of the office, his back to them. Latif and Jeg were also in shock, they had not known how chaotic Alhaji had planned to turn the country into. They were also surprised at the swift response from the Nigerian military. This was something they never anticipated will happen. Latif and Jeg began to whisper to each other while Bisi and Ufan just sat down and watched the President nervously.

'what is the population of the area'? the President asked without looking back. The minister stood up and walked to meet him; he put his hand on his shoulders and said softly.

'you don't need to worry Mr. President, it's in the outskirts of Kantagora. There were reported gunshots coming out from the area which made us positioned our satellite in that direction and the satellite images gathered so far, have shown us the exact spot of the hideout.'

The President raised his head and stared at him

'from what we gathered' the minister continued; 'we only have three or four hostages; the team will enter in the night and swipe the area clean before morning.'

'please Mr. President if I may say something'. Bisi was saying.

The President turned round and began to walk back to his desk. He came to rest on the desk and leaned his back to it facing the ladies.

'you were saying…..'

'our fiancées are there, held hostages. We are not selfish but please whatever you do; we need them back home alive'.

Ufan swallowed deep as they watched the President ponder over the issue.

'there is something else Mr. President'. the NSA said; the President turned to look at him as if surprise to see him inside his office.

'Ayo and Nosa are military'. Bisi and Ufan looked at each other and stared at the NSA chief.

'pardon me sir, but what did you just say'? Ufan was saying.

The NSA smiled and turned his attention to the President.

'these boys were trained by me when I was in the Nigerian Defense Academy. They passed out normally just as the other regulars but somehow, they opted out for civilian life style after their peace keeping mission in Liberia.'

'as for the Bamidele mentioned in the letter' the minister was saying; 'from investigations and from what the captured gunman has revealed to us, he is one of us.' Latif and Jeg sat up.

'he is military too; he was posted as an undercover agent to the Edo state Police Headquarters. The sister was later kidnapped by Alhaji Abudu who made him to work for him before the sister can be released to him. Bamidele has tried contacting us but the trails he left were inconclusive hence we sort of lost contact with him.'

Chief Latif opened his mouth and tried to say something but the President held up his hand.

'don't bother chief Latif, I authorized that and it wasn't to indict you or something. The military has an undercover agent all over the police force'.

The chief's mouth was still opened. He looked at Jeg in shock and disbelief. Jeg too was in shock over the Minister's utterances but they kept mute and waited for the President's decision.

'as military', the minister continued; 'they ought to be able to take care of themselves but our boys have orders to look out for them when they swipe the place. But the funny thing is Ayo and Nosa don't know of Bamidele's loyalty'.

'okay' the President said with a deep sigh;

'send in the boys. I want this operation done quietly with minimal casualties but I want that goat alive.'

The defense minister nodded.

'for your information sir', he said; 'the operation has been tagged operation Katangora'.

The President went back to his chair to sit down just then a tap came on the door.

An SSS man came in and walked straight to the minister of defense. He whispered something into his ears and went out. Everyone in the office focus their attention on him. The minister smiled, he looked up at the President and said;

'I guess our work has been simplified'.

'what was it'? the President asked.

'the air force has just intercepted a helicopter carrying Bamidele and the sister. They also have your fiancées in custody' he said looking at Bisi and Ufan.

Both girls screamed and jumped up but when they realized where they were, they hush their tones and hugged themselves with excitement.

'where are they now'? the President asked

'they are flying them to defense headquarters for debriefing sir'.

'well, I guess it's almost over now' Latif was saying casually.

'it's your problem now' the President said pointing to the NSA and the minister of defense,

'bring me news and call me the information minister; let's see how we can manage the media angle'.

They got up and the defense minister led the way out of the President's office. They went through the glass door and came into the large hall. Apart from the eight SSS men mounting the different sections of the hall and the fat man sitting behind the big desk, the hall was empty. The politicians must have been dispersed Ufan thought. The minister brought out his phone and dialed a number;

'operation Katangora is a go boys' he said and cut the line.

At this point, the NSA turned round to face chief Latif and said;

'thank you very much Chief Latif, the nation is indebted to you and Jegbefo. I will make the necessary recommendations to the President; he then looked at Bisi and Ufan, he shook their hands and said;

'as for you two, well, you've done your best for this country and I'll see to it that your wishes are taken care of. You'll be hearing from us soon.'

'how soon can we see them'? Ufan was asking

'very soon' the minister said smiling.

'once we do the debriefing, we'll release them to you. You girls can go home now hmmm, we'll do the cleaning up okay'?

Chief Latif smiled and shook their hands. The two SSS men that initially led them into the villa appeared again and led them out to the helipad where the chopper was waiting. They happily got in and the chopper took off.

Printed by Libri Plureos GmbH in Hamburg, Germany